Chump Change

DAN FANTE was born and raised in Los Angeles. At twenty, he quit school and hit the road, eventually ending up as a New York City resident for 12 years. Fante has worked at dozens of crummy jobs including: door to door salesman, taxi driver, window washer, telemarketer, private investigator, night hotel manager, chauffeur, mail-room clerk, deck hand, dishwasher, carnival barker, envelope stuffer, dating service counselor, furniture salesman, and parking attendant. He hopes eventually to meet a fat waitress and learn to play the harmonica.

Chump Change

Dan Fante

First published in the UK in 1999
by Rebel Inc, an imprint of Canongate Books Ltd,
14 High Street, Edinburgh EH1 1TE.

First published by Pavillons in France, with the title
Les Anges N'ont Rien Dans les Poches.

10 9 8 7 6 5 4 3 2 1

Rebel Inc series editor: Kevin Williamson
www.rebelinc.net

British Library Cataloguing-in-Publication Data
A catalogue record for this book is available upon request
from the British Library.

ISBN 0 86241 958 1

Typeset by Palimpsest Book Production Limited,
Polmont, Stirlingshire
Printed and bound by
Creative Print and Design (Wales), Ebbw Vale.

This book is dedicated to:

Freddie Free Base
Liquor-Store Dave
TJ Bratter
Bob A.
Bassia Loebel
Elinor Blake
Billy-Fucking-Childish
and all the gentlemen who congregate at Roxbury Park.

And, of course, to John Fante, my father, whose brilliance and memory are my constant inspiration.

'Think dyin's tough . . .
Dyin' ain't shit
The hard part is living
While the dying's going on.'

Something I heard TJ say

Chapter One

MY NAME IS BRUNO Dante and what I'm writing about here is what happened. On December 4th, the St. Joseph of Cupertino Hospital alcohol and nut ward in the Bronx, on Mosholu Parkway, let me go. Released me, again. Each time I took their twenty-eight-day cure I found out how much their in-patient charges went up. This last time, I stabbed myself in a blackout and they almost wouldn't accept me as a patient. This last time was the worst, because all that I could remember seeing when I came around was the blood gushing out of my stomach onto my clothes.

My first recovery at St. Joe's was paid for by my wife Agnes's insurance from her job. It worked okay. Then two years went by, with some shrink work, and it happened again – a ten-day drunk and another suicide attempt. Booze and coke. By the second stay, the cost had increased from eighty-five hundred dollars to twelve thousand dollars, and that time the fee came out of our pocket – thought we still had money in the bank then. I stopped the shrink because I was still drinking and not getting any better. This cure, the third, I was a charity case. It would have cost twenty-five K.

When I drink for too many days in a row, especially wine, I think too much and my mind wants to kill me. This last time, in a county shithole, my bed was bolted to the floor and I was strapped to it. Normal people don't get locked up in detox. And the average person won't end up with a knife in his stomach tomorrow morning. But I have these consciousness lapses, and more and more in those lapses, I do behavior that I can't remember. They're blackouts. I know what they are. Then Agnes had me transferred to St. Joe's.

My behavior is often extreme and destructive and happens because I am unable to tolerate myself when I'm sober – after I remember or find out what I've done on a binge. So I drink again to fix that. Like I said, mostly wine because regular alcohol stopped getting me off quite a while ago. I only drink regular booze to maintain. The last year or so it's only the wine that gets me to the other side.

This time, wine and sex set off the insanity which led to the suicide attempt. I'm not a homosexual, but I was out of control, blasted on Mad Dog 20-20 in a porno movie on Fourteenth Street. I allowed two guys to watch while I fucked this other guy. They were jerking each other off. Stuff like that. I was in and out of consciousness but I remember most of what took place. I don't know why I did it, except that I must have wanted to. That night I used the steak knife on myself.

The cures have no lasting effect. They'll help for a while. I'll stay away from wine for weeks or months and just drink booze, but then something will happen in my head and I'll be off again.

What I want to say here is that there is a place beyond control and beyond concern that people can go, where the values and the needs of everyday life change completely. Where what matters is moment-to-moment survival to avoid mind pain.

Delbert was in the nut house with me. I'll tell about him here. We were roommates there for three weeks. He's a guy from Lubbock, Texas who ended up in Accounts Payable in a Wall Street company. He has this family with 2.1 kids and a wife that cooks dinner. How it happens in specific detail is not important, but Delbert comes home every day and goes to work like he is supposed to, and he does this for ten years or so. He is unhappy with problems like everybody gets, so he drinks at lunch sometimes and then goes home and sits in front of the TV at night and drinks some more. On weekends he drinks too. But it stayed under control for many years. Delbert is like everybody else. He is no different. He is a working guy. A family man. One day, he notices that he needs to drink in the morning just to keep his nerves steady. He doesn't want the lady at the ticket booth in the Long Island Railroad to see him shake when he buys his ticket, or the secretaries at the office to notice he has a problem when he pours his office coffee. So he becomes a morning drinker out of necessity.

Then, after work one night, Del comes home a bit toasted and has another argument with the old lady about his drinking. (What I'm saying here is average stuff. It happens to normal people.) He leaves and goes to the bar and comes back completely shit-faced at 2:00 a.m. and gets in bed with his ten-year-old daughter, Melissa. He doesn't know the difference. Awake and sober, it would be incomprehensible to him to be on top of his own daughter, fucking her and hurting her. The wife hears the noises and finds them there.

Delbert is sorry and his insurance pays for him to come to St. Joseph of Cupertino's detox. He didn't know why he let it go this far. Didn't really think himself capable of sliding his dick deeply into his daughter's little body.

Can Delbo forgive himself? Apparently not, because he hung himself last week and is now dead.

That night I had dozed off and woke up again at four-thirty to take a piss. Delbert was not in his bed across from mine. I walked down the corridor past the rec room to the bathrooms. I knew that he was upset working through the shame and the truth that he was a daughter-rapist and an alcoholic.

The rec room door is always kept closed because patients are not allowed in, except when the room is supervised. There's Delbert. He's slashed his wrists and hung himself at the same time. Blood everywhere. Before lights-out, we were discussing the playoffs. He was a committed Cowboys fan. So long, Delbert.

My wife, Agnes, arrived to pick me up in a cab. Two days early. She hates me and our marriage, but is never late for anything. It was a checker taxi and it was waiting outside with the meter running.

I said goodbye to Ed D., Capgun Steve and the other guys standing around while the cabbie slammed my stuff in the trunk. Ed made 'V's' with both hands and held them up like an imitation of Nixon. We shook hands and said, 'See ya.'

Agnes didn't talk at all as we drove. I smoked and watched the Grand Concourse roll by for ten minutes before she told me that Jonathan Dante, my father, was dying in L.A. from failed kidneys and diabetes and that was the reason I was released early from treatment. He'd been at home in my mother's care after a second leg amputation, when his old, abused, blind diabetic body decided to give out and quit. His remains were in ICU at Cedars in serious condition.

Agnes and I had been married for eleven years. She was a teacher and the daughter of Jewish parents from the Bronx. Black eyes and black hair and a wonderful ass like the pillow of an angel. We met one night at a poetry reading on Second Avenue when I was still writing.

I had read two of my published things, short angry pieces. She found them good and had asked a colleague literature teacher to put us together, which she had. Aggie thought that poets drinking tequila were romantic, so we went back to my room to discuss W.B. Yeats.

We lived together after that, and I worked and she worked, and for most of the time, while I was still writing at night, things were okay. But I had frequent headaches and depression about my poetry and low income from dismal-paying shit jobs. I was overly critical and cruel to Agnes, so I self-prescribed whiskey to pick up my spirits, and discovered that the depressions lessened when I drank and didn't write. I stopped criticizing Agnes, but I also stopped caring.

About that time, I got a temp job in telephone sales and found I had a knack for it. Soon I was bringing in good money. It changed everything. The depression and migraines subsided, cured by the excitement of success. I forgot about writing altogether.

In a year, I had opened my own phone room selling porno videos with a partner. One weekend, Agnes and I got married in Maryland. I promised her that I would go back to writing, which was a lie because, by then, I was pulling in five grand a week, sometimes more. I burned out at selling porn videos and eventually moved on to feature knockoffs. Six months here, one year there, working the phone four or five hours a day. I always became a top guy wherever I went. My worst month, I brought home twice what Aggie made as a teacher.

Over the next few years, I sold office supplies, computer ribbon, cable and wire, guaranteed loans, tools, ad space, and oil and gas leases. When one deal got slow, I went on to the next.

At the end of my shifts, in the afternoon, I got in the habit of stopping at the bar. At first it was with the other phone room people, out-of-work actors and musicians, people like me making their living hustling. We snorted a lot of coke and pissed our money away. Then gradually, over time, the depressions came back, the boozing got worse, and I became a morning drinker too.

I opened another bucket shop. This time on my own. Office supplies. After three months, my top guy sent an eight hundred dollar, 27″ color TV to a department manager of a company. He got caught receiving the bribe by his supervisor. His boss told the Attorney General's office, and three weeks later we were shut down. They locked my door and seized my inventory. I lost sixty thousand dollars.

That was the year I started entering treatment facilities for alcohol and insanity and I had my first suicide attempt.

The marriage had been over for a while, but neither one of us talked about it. Aggie began paying the apartment rent by herself. I tried boiler rooms again, but I was drinking hard and I would come in late, lose time from work, and eventually get fired. After that, I stayed home collecting unemployment when I could get it.

I wanted to write, but there was nothing there. No interest. And I had lost the ability to concentrate. I was a drunk. I knew it and there was nothing I could do about it.

As the cab headed south on the Grand Concourse, Aggie presented me with the information about my father, like a reporter doing a toxic waste story for a TV news broadcast. She had begun to enjoy delivering dispassionate facts about my life, wearing rubber gloves as she discussed anything to do with me. The death data about the old man came rattling out, and I learned all the medical terms and probabilities for his survival. It was cold stuff. I could tell that she hated my guts and wanted no more of me.

Aggie had discovered that the way to cope with me was through Valium. I could always tell when she was whacked because her speech was thick and her spit pasty.

I tried looking at her, but she wouldn't look back. She was talking to the rear of the driver's seat, below the bulletproof partition, where there were theater posters displayed. Her words were coming out in measured, fortified calmness, and she seemed to be absorbed in the old City Of Angels ad more than the other two signs.

She'd been having an affair with a colleague for almost three years. A PE teacher. I knew about it. His nickname was Buddy. Bernard Williams. An ex-basketball nigger from NYU. Six-foot-five-inches tall. I didn't mind the black part that much, what I hated was the mendacity and deception. The ease with which she backed away from our marriage.

Agnes started with the guy while I was in the hospital for my second trip. I got home after twenty-eight days and was instructed to sleep in the living room on the hide-a-bed. She'd lock the door to our bedroom as she'd go in and out. She announced that she had taken a job at night and would be coming home late.

In a few days, I figured the deal out, but the shame of a beaten dog kept me quiet. I was the reprobate husband. The bad guy. Agnes was paying the bills so I'd lost my right to complain. It was my choice, I could sleep on the couch or in the street.

At first, watching her affair tore my guts out. But then it became a reason to drink. I knew she was getting even, like the time she burned the only copies of several dozen of my original poems because, once more, on a binge, I had stayed away for a week.

There was rage and depression. Once or twice, drunk, I confronted her about Buddy, but all she did was lock herself in the bedroom and call the police.

We crossed the bridge at the end of the Grand Concourse and the cabbie swung onto the Harlem River Parkway, then picked up the FDR Drive. Ten minutes later, we were at Sixtieth Street and Second Avenue, a cross-town street, two short blocks from our apartment.

I wanted to *feel* about my old man. To have a reaction to the news of his imminent death. I waited for an emotion, but it didn't come. I was surprised by my numbness. Then I realized that I had come to care about nothing.

The cabbie pulled to the curb and got out to get my bag from the trunk. Agnes was keeping the cab and going on to work. 'Do you realize that you haven't spoken a word to me this whole ride?' she said.

I got out, too, but before I closed the door I leaned my head back inside. I said, 'Thanks for picking me up.'

The cabbie was behind the wheel again.

'That's it?' she said.

'I said "thank you."'

'Fuck you, mister.'

I watched the cab pull away and picked up my bag and walked back uptown toward our apartment.

It was cold for December. Maybe fifteen degrees. I didn't want to call California to find out if my father was alive or dead. I didn't want to know. I hadn't had a drink in twenty-six days.

I dropped my stuff and walked back across town toward the Lexington Avenue subway and the liquor store. There was a choice to make – I was owed two checks at the unemployment office, but I was almost out of cigarettes and there wasn't enough money in my pocket for subway fare to go downtown, get cigarettes, and also buy a half pint of Ten-High to hold me over until I got the checks. I needed the drink right away, cigarettes could wait. No choice after all.

I phoned. Jonathan Dante wasn't dead yet. We would make the trip.

Agnes took her Valium for air travel too. Planes scared her, so out came the blue bombers. By the time our cab had gone from mid-town to Kennedy Airport for the 1:00 p.m. flight to L.A., the two she'd taken with breakfast had kicked in. Wobbling and walking, she followed me through the terminal, then nodded off while we were waiting to board the plane.

As soon as we were in our seats and the plane was off the ground, Aggie was asleep again. I knew that she'd be out for hours. It was fine with me. I folded both trays down and ordered two sets of double Jack Daniels' and paid with a ten dollar bill from my wife's purse.

The flight wasn't crowded and all the seats near us were empty except for another couple seated two rows forward. The stewardess's name was Lorette.

I ordered more drinks. When Lorette came back with them, I ordered more and hammered the first four, over ice. Right away I began feeling at ease and my mind calmed down.

When Lorette came again, I ordered another set of doubles and paid with my own money this time. A fifty-dollar bill. I did it because I noticed that the top button of her blouse was unbuttoned as she bent down to collect the empties. I smiled. She smiled back. I wanted her to see the big bill. We were having a nice exchange. Polite. Two Americans. Travelers.

'Your wife went right to sleep. Want a pillow?'

'No. That's not necessary. She's comfortable. Flying bothers her so she takes tranquilizers.' There was a nice tan line halfway down Lorette's left breast. Her lipstick was very red.

'Oh, a fifty . . . Anything smaller?'

I could feel the Jack taking the edge off, smoothing out my nervousness. All that I actually had to do was reach into Agnes's purse again, but I wanted Lorette to see my roll. To observe that I was a player with my unemployment money.

So, shifting my weight, I reached into my pants' pocket

again and pulled out the rest of the hundreds, all carefully folded with the heads in one direction. 'Let's see,' I said, fanning the money open on the fold-down table, so we could both examine the spread. Making sure that she saw how many there were, I announced, 'That looks to be the smallest I've got. Sorry.'

'That's a nice problem to have.'

'Thank you, you're nice too,' I said.

Lorette took the fifty and said that she would return with the change after she had finished serving the other passengers. Before she walked away, she smiled again and looked down at the eight full miniatures and the eight empties. 'Are these all for you?'

I smiled back. 'Not exactly. I like the bottles,' I said, lying like a fool.

When she'd gone, I stowed all the small, full bottles, except the last four, in the inside pocket of my jacket. Those I opened individually, sucking out the contents of each into my mouth.

I felt okay, except as I was looking out the window, watching Manhattan fade, I was suddenly choked by a sadness. A thought, then a feeling. Twirling across my mind like a silent ballerina.

I looked over at my unconscious wife to make sure I was alone and private and safe. I was. Then I let myself feel what was there. Tears came and there was a convulsion in my gut.

The full power of the Jack hadn't kicked in yet, and a clear image of my father came to me. My favorite photograph of him. I hadn't seen it in years, but my mind brought it back clearly. Dante was no more than twenty-two or twenty-three years old, standing on a lawn in a sweaty T-shirt, the hot sun at his back, pants rolled up from playing baseball, hands on his hips and his head cocked to one side, looking insolently into the camera. A proud, defiant young Dante with the world by the balls. More tears came.

In a little while, I got up and made a tour of the plane, passing the galley and winding up at the aircraft's rear bathrooms. There was a kid in front of me waiting his turn.

We talked because he wanted to talk. He was twelve years old and filled with answers and statistics regarding all sorts of things about air travel. Flight time based on wind resistance, which planes had what passenger capacities. Idiot shit. Stuff that no one cares about except twelve-year-old boys. I listened to the poetry of his numbers, the DC-10 and the 747, the Stealth Bomber and the Space Shuttle. The magic of his first flight had his mind staggered with possibility and amazement. A DC-10 airplane was a love sonnet, a Degas painting.

The kid seemed to be the ghost of my not-yet-dead father from the photograph, speaking back to me from fifty years ago, carrying some confused message to the present about energy and hope. But I knew it was probably the whiskey.

The boy went on and on and I began to cry. I didn't care.

The same wave of terrible sadness hit me again. Grief for the defiant, uncrushed spirit of my old man as he was in the picture. Dante's ghost resisting time and challenging death.

Then the bathroom door swung open and a lady came out and passed us. The boy stepped inside but whispered back to me before he closed the door, 'Mister, are you scared too? Of airplanes?'

I looked at him. 'I guess I am,' I said.

'We won't fall. I promise. My dad says it's aerodynamically impossible.'

'That's good to know. Thanks.'

I got back to my seat. The Jack had me now, fully, transforming the knives in my brain into pillows. I relaxed. The ride to L.A.

would be comfortable. Aggie would sleep. Soon they'd bring the food, I could watch a movie and have a few more drinks. The rawness about Jonathan Dante had faded.

Lorette was making her way down the aisle with the food service cart. She was ten or fifteen rows away, but I could easily make out her firm calf muscles flexing as she stooped down to fetch food trays and plastic cups and fill them with Diet Cokes or club soda. She had an abundant hipline and a firm-looking puff-butt. The top button on her blouse was still unbuttoned.

I watched as she slowly worked her cart back toward my row, and I cleared off a magazine and some empty miniatures on my fold-down table to make room for my order of more drinks when she arrived.

Her heavy wagon was half a dozen passengers away. A thought came to me, and I slid my wife's coat across from her seat to cover my lap. Then, as I watched Lorette moved closer, I unzipped my fly. My dick was hard right away. As I worked my hand up and down, I watched Lorette being congenial and dispensing food and wine and diet soda and booze six rows away. Now five.

Something distracted her and she looked back over the seat tops in my direction. She was smiling her accommodating smile. Our eyes didn't meet, but I noticed to my pleasure that another of her blouse buttons had worked its way open. A lower button. Fifth from the top. My cock was iron.

The sweetness of the Kentucky whiskey had me free from the fear that my wife would wake up and see me. There were four rows between me and Lorette's cart. Rows without passengers. She was on her way back to me. The heavy cart clunked slowly. Three rows. Two. I had to grab the cocktail napkins off the tray and fan them open with my free hand. They were wadded around my dick when I came. *Wham! Wham! Wham!*

A second later she was above me with the cart. 'Lunch?'she said smiling, setting two plates of food down on the opened tray tables and counting out my change from the fifty that I had paid her with before.

'Good idea. Thanks,' I said back with my own smile, feeling the relief of the orgasm.

When she had rolled her cart past, I withdrew the soaked napkins from under the coat. They were heavy with cum. Then I moved my food and pushed the tray table up and checked for stains. There weren't any, so I put my dick away and zipped up my fly.

Next to me was my wife, asleep, peaceful, stoned, sucking air in and out through thick, parted lips. Then I was seized with a perverse idea. An even-steven for her and her boyfriend – for not having given me head in the last five years and opening her legs to a trespasser.

I unfolded the saturated napkins with the goo in the middle and dipped two fingers into the wet paste. I brought them up quickly to Aggie's mouth, then wiped the cum generously across her puffy lips, even rolling one finger around inside in the lower crevice between the lip and teeth. The action forced a reflex from my wife – she licked her mouth. After that, I buried the wet napkins in her purse and ate both lunches.

Chapter Two

SEEING L.A. FROM the air was more frightening than memory permitted. Real, vivid, science fiction. It was just after sundown when we began to land. The natural light of day was gone, replaced by billions of smog particles that gave the coming darkness the hue of blood in a draining sink. This enormous, overfed, infected pink pig of a city rolled across the landscape as far as the eye could see, coughing, snorting and sucking up whatever was once natural and undisturbed.

As the plane descended over the clogged freeways I felt eaten, swallowed within the canopy of filth. A primal instinct warned me that being here was a mistake. Demands would be required of me that I was unprepared to fulfill. The darkness here was too large to defend against.

When we'd landed and I woke Agnes up, we got off the plane and made our way to the baggage claim turnstiles to wait for my brother, Fabrizio. I'd forgotten about the long halls and moving walkways. Suddenly, my mind clicked on like a screaming monkey. Then the body craved booze. I was starting to sweat and feel dizzy.

I left Agnes there by the shiny rotating suitcase conveyor belt. In the bathroom, I pumped handfuls of water up to my face and felt the coldness counteracting my perspiration. Then I checked my appearance. What I saw made me sneer. The guy in the mirror was an impostor. The business suit and tie were absurd and excessive. I still could not give up trying to show them that I was okay. Why did I care? They already knew that my life was coming apart.

I was decomposing from within, like this preposterous town. L.A. was the right place for me after all. I belonged here with the killers of my father: the mind-fucking twenty-two-year-old movie producers and distribution gurus who'd dictated the course of his life. I was a true son of L.A.

This was perfect. In a drunken sexual frenzy, I had disgraced myself, then cut my wrists in jail, and now I would show up to shake my brother's hand and kiss my mother's cheek.

Standing there I made a decision. I didn't care. There had been far too many stupid attempts to please others. There would be no more personal requital. My father had spent his life saying the right thing, and ass-kissing actors and Hollywood agents, and now he'd be dead for his trouble. It had never made him happy. I was what I was.

I dried my face. I wasn't sorry. Then I went outside to the baggage area to find my brother and my wife.

The given name on his birth certificate was Fabrizio. My father immediately regretted the choice as too affected for a writer's son and too ethnic for Southern California, so a few days later, he changed it to Thomas. Tommy. But they never changed it legally.

I liked the name Fabrizio. It was off-beat and clumsy. I was twelve when he was born, and I chose to continue to call him Fabrizio when we were alone. Not Tommy. The old man told me to stop, but I never did. It stuck as a secret affection between me and the kid. To me, he was Fabrizio.

We were opposites, physically. My hair was light. I was short and thick like my father, with his eyes and nose and chin, but fair-skinned like my mother. Fabrizio was dark like the old man, with wavy Wop hair, but with slim and gentle anglo features like his mother.

We were amalgams of cross-breeding, what happens when a woman of English-German upper middle class ancestry marries an olive-skinned, thick-fingered, Italian bricklayer's son.

I had left Malibu for New York City when Fabrizio was twelve, and the kid had come to view me as kind of a half-parent. While he was growing up, I was frequently the subject of conversation at my family's dinner table. He learned about the large amounts of money that I earned and spent in my varied telemarketing business ventures. Later, as reports of arrests and suicide attempts were repeated, his opinion of me changed. Now he would look at me much as my wife did, like a lab animal.

Fab was twenty-five now and a USC graduate in economics. He still had the same car from eight years before. A 1970 Ford Country Squire wagon with the monster four-sixty motor that he'd rebuilt himself. He was dating the same two girls from high school.

We loaded the bags into the Country Squire and headed north toward Malibu. From Fab I learned that my father's condition was unchanged. His kidneys had failed irreversibly, and the doctors were predicting death within a day or two.

It was seven p.m. and the heat from the day kept the air warm. Fab and Agnes talked while I smoked in the back seat with the window down.

There were cars and clothing named after Malibu. TV shows. Years before, when I first arrived in New York, people had odd reactions to the information that I was from Malibu. I learned that I came from a place that people went to, but weren't supposed to leave. New Yorkers looked at me like I was an animated Disney character. After the first conversations, I stopped talking about where I was from. If somebody asked where I grew up I'd say, 'L.A.'

One night, two weeks after I'd arrived in New York, drunk in a bar on First Avenue, I bet a guy who had a sister in Pomona that there were statues of movie stars all over Los Angeles. The Emilio Estevez was in Santa Monica and the Peter Graves was in Glendale. Vincent Price, before he died, had a chain of California discount stores named after him.

As we made the drive north up the Coast Highway I remembered things. Landmarks. I tried to estimate how many times I had passed Gladstones' Restaurant. Five thousand times? Ten thousand?

I recalled the photographs of what my father's house had been like over thirty years before – a big Y-shaped ranch-style deal standing alone near a windy cliff eight miles past the Malibu Colony.

There were no housing developments or banks out that far in those days, and the nearest market was almost halfway back to Santa Monica. I remembered noticing as a boy, when I scrambled up on the roof to shag a stray baseball, that the closest house was half-a-mile away. Our place was built on a spur of land jutting out into the Pacific Ocean where the Indians had buried their dead two hundred years before – named after the French explorer, Dume. Pronounced Doom.

From Torrance or Redondo Beach looking north, the last point of land visible is the hill named Point Dume, flat-topped since WW II when the War Department gave it a crewcut in preparation to make it a strategic gun emplacement. But the 'Yellow Menace' from the east never arrived, and twenty years later, Jonathan Dante bought one of the four haciendas on the barren land.

In the 1950's, the afternoon winds would howl across the flatlands and tumbleweeds blew off the cliffs and hang-glided to the sea a hundred feet below. You could hear seals barking on the rocks and from time to time, around the end of the point, a tribe of whales would chug by, gasping spray twenty feet into the air on their way to warmer waters in Mexico.

Movie money had purchased the Dante home. My father, who at twenty-one had hitchhiked to L.A. from Boulder with three dollars in his pocket, had become a rich screenwriter. He had heeded the advice of his mentor, H.L. Mencken, who years before, had told him to 'take every cent they'll pay you.'

After six months in L.A., young Jonathan Dante was rotting in a hotel room on Bunker Hill, unable to finish his novel, broke and weeks behind on his rent. Mencken exhorted him to take the gig.

It was only a two-week assignment. A writer friend of my father's who knew his short story work and was pulling down fat weekly paychecks at RKO, recommended they hire the old man to re-write a court scene in a John Garfield flick. The job paid five-hundred a week. Enough to finance Dante's novel for another six months. He grabbed up the quick money and for the rest of his life served two masters.

What happened to Jonathan Dante in Los Angeles is what happens to a man who falls in love with a beautiful, heartless bitch. Each time you touch her round hard breasts and press yourself deeply between her legs, rapture explodes your heart. Possessing her flawlessness fills you with a drug, a perfect divine bliss. You have a dick that never gets soft. The paychecks, the kisses fix everything.

He didn't look forward or back anymore because he'd learned that in Hollywood the *now* is all that counts. He forgot that his passion was writing novels. He took up golf. Covering the nut and nights drinking at Musso's with his screenwriter pals, became what mattered. After that, his preoccupations became rewrite deadlines and stocks and real estate and the putting green at Fox Hills.

L.A. was a flawless plum of a town then. Wonderful big open streets and crisp, dry air and an endless sun that filled the world with hope. Her people were open and friendly and the picture business brought a dream-come-true reality to the place that was unavoidable. It really could happen. You could move west to L.A. and change your life. Southern California was FDR's prototype of the New Deal.

A poor writer growing up in the poverty of the thirties, finding L.A. blooming, beautiful – an air-brushed kibbutz paradise – Dante knew he must have her and let his tongue penetrate her every orifice. At the time it didn't matter too much that, in the essence of his bones, he knew he was licking the clit of the spider lady.

Chapter Three

TWENTY MINUTES PAST Sunset Boulevard, we turned off the Coast Highway onto Heathercliff Road. The personalized license plate on the Benz convertible in front of us read, 'SE ME WIN.' I knew I was home.

When we pulled into the driveway we could see that the house was completely dark. Fab said Mom was at the hospital with my sister and my sister's husband, Benny Roth.

I got out to open the big iron gate and flipped the latch and pushed it open a few feet, less than wide enough to admit Fab's station wagon.

A rusty hinge creaked in the darkness. A kind of low groan. Something within made me restrain myself from opening it all the way.

Then a second later, I knew why. In the distance I heard growling and the moonlight revealed a hairy white torpedo of a dog coming around the corner. It was my father's pride and joy, his husky fourteen-year-old bull terrier, Rocco. What Jake La Motta had been to middleweight fighters, Rocco was once to other dogs. As he got closer I could see his limp, and the ancient, jagged scars covering his face. Dried rivers of pain from a hundred wars.

His head bore the marks of the population growth of our family's neighborhood. Like the rings of age in the center of a tree, each scar corresponded with the new arrival of a Doberman, a rottweiler, a German shepherd or a Great

Dane. He'd fought them all as their masters built homes and eventually made the error of letting their dogs pass the perimeter of my father's driveway. Rocco's face was the record.

The dog got to within a couple of feet of me, then stopped and stood his ground. He was checking me out. I waited. He wasn't growling any more, so I tentatively reached out to pet him.

Rocco grabbed my sleeved arm playfully, like a Kung-Fu master demonstrating a lethal thrust to an eight-year-old. Then he let it go. I allowed him complete control.

Aggie and I got inside and unpacked in the bedroom that had once belonged to Fabrizio and me. There were still two double beds in the room. Not joined. Agnes was content with the sleeping arrangements.

Fab wanted to know if I was going to return to the hospital with him that night to be with the old man. I did not want to go and my kid brother, knowing that I'd just come out of a treatment facility and trying not to pressure me, gave me the option of staying at the house. I didn't want to see the old man. Not yet. Rather than be with me, Agnes decided to accompany my brother to the hospital. I would have the house to myself.

After they'd gone, I went into the kitchen to check the liquor supply. There was a counter-top full of whiskey and vodka bottles. I poured myself a glass and walked out on the cliff to smoke and drink with the night. The ghosts of dead dogs and the whispering of my old man's voice in my head kept me company.

One hundred feet below, I could make out a waveless beach in the moonlight and feel the dry breeze of a Santa Ana wind moving in from the east.

I was sure that I didn't belong here, and I recognized that the familiarity of that feeling repeated my sensation of strangeness and separateness, one I always had in the hospital treatment center. It was the same experience I had been having in my own apartment with my wife. I understood that I had become uncomfortable with all of my life, *everywhere*.

It was surely part of the reason that my drinking had gotten out of control. Knowing that information made me further realize that I had come to completely not give a shit about anything. The Jack Daniels and the wine took the edge off that truth. It was why I was unwilling to quit.

The smell of the ocean was everywhere, as I stood on the cliff looking out. Nothing was really different here, except everything. It all looked the same, except it had all changed.

In the morning Agnes was asleep and I found a note from Fabrizio. She and my brother had returned after midnight from the hospital, then he had gone home to Santa Monica.

The note said that the old man was worse, being kept alive by a drug that made his kidneys function, but pneumonia had set in. Our mother had spent the night with him at the ICU. Jonathan Dante would not live another day.

I had been up since before dawn, sweating and smoking cigarettes, roaming the large empty house with the peopleless rooms. When the daylight came, I was standing at the kitchen sink making coffee, looking north out the window. In the half-light of day I could see that there was even more new construction. The housing depression of the nineties had avoided Point Dume. Squinting to see further down the road, I recognized where a large gully and a creek bed with boulders and jagged rock formations had once existed. It was gone. Covered over. A green-mirrored house on stilts was in its place. Expensive.

In the bathroom I puked, showered, and continued to add fingers of whiskey to my coffee until some of my trembling went away. It bothered me that my shakes had returned so soon after going almost a month of detoxing without a drink. When I'd soothed the tremors enough, I managed to reset my watch. I'd slept a total of two hours.

As I was shaving, I heard Fab arrive and enter the house through the door to the back porch. He called, 'Anybody home,' but I didn't answer. The eyes that I saw looking back at me in the bathroom mirror were those of a dog loose on the freeway.

We drank coffee together standing in the kitchen. He wanted to know what had happened to me. Why had I landed in the nut ward? He was a very intense guy, and his directness came from a fear that what I had might be inherited by him too.

I had not planned to be crazy, I said. Arrests for lewd practices in public were things that happened when I drank. I'd not planned on being a degenerate. Life got away from me. Out of hand. I couldn't figure it out either.

But I was his brother and he wanted to know why I let other men suck my dick. I could tell that he'd decided that I was irresponsible and selfish and that my problems stemmed from a lack of self-discipline. I drank too much and I let myself rum amuck. That was my problem.

We talked about him too. Fab was proud that he had put himself through college and into grad school mostly from working in a supermarket. When the old man had gotten sick and his only income had been his Social Security and Writers Guild Pension, my brother had paid for his education by himself. At one store, working his way up from box boy to checker to assistant manager. Union wages. Vacations. Dental benefits. Six years at USC. The CPA exam.

*　　　*　　　*

I convinced Fab to let Agnes sleep while he and I drove to Cedars. He knew Aggie and I weren't getting along. For days he had been dutifully shuttling back and forth from Malibu to Santa Monica to get my sister, then back to the hospital in his Country Squire. Running errands for our mother, picking up medicine. Coping with the old man's condition by staying busy. As we backed out of the driveway and pointed the car toward L.A., he passed me his watch. It was digital and had a stopwatch function.

He wanted me to help him time our drive. It was a sort of game. To keep himself interested and occupied during his trips to the hospital, he timed each of his runs.

So when Fab said 'GO,' I pressed the black button on the side of the watch and we peeled out.

While we drove, he wanted to tell me about his lifestyle. How he'd gotten the MBA through hard work and determination. It was a lecture on how I personally could be more responsible. I put the window down and smoked and watched the digits of his stopwatch speeding in a mechanical frenzy while he yacked on about himself.

Fitness was a primary factor for Fab. A positive mental attitude was important also. 'What we think about is who we are.'

Furthermore, he explained what had caused our father's health to fail. The perils of too much salt and fat and cholesterol. Stress. And piss-poor financial planning.

Fab reminded me that Dante had squandered hundreds of thousands during the many years he had worked as a screenwriter in L.A. It was harsh, but he had to admit that the old man was a careless, selfish fool. He whispered these words and shook his head sadly.

To Fab, the solutions were clear then, just as they were today. Dante should have bought property. He'd be rich. Trust deeds alone could have assured a comfortable retirement. Now, on his death bed, to my brother's shock, Mom had disclosed that the old man had made no provisions for his heirs whatever. There was no will.

Fifteen minutes into the ride, I felt myself getting sick to my stomach. The self-righteous crap coming from him was forcing a pool of bile to collect at the bottom of my throat. I was sweating, soaking through the back of my shirt. Completely out of patience.

Each judgmental, pissy remark and criticism about our father made me want to grab handfuls of his hair out by the roots. Each sound, each resonating shit-filled emission of his speaking increased my edginess.

For a minute, I was distracted as we passed the La Costa area, where the scars of the last big fire had not yet healed. I could see that everything on the hills had been obliterated. Denise Jacobson, a junior high school friend, had bought a house there after college and a divorce. It had been destroyed.

Stumps of other expensive homes stood like seared head-stone reminders of the equality of cataclysm. Saigon must have looked like this after it was overrun. South Central L.A. God doled out pain with impersonal indifference.

By the time we got to the Topanga area on the Coast Highway, I could take Fabrizio no more. 'Let's pull in at the market,' I blurted, interrupting his monologue. 'I need cigarettes.'

'No stopping,' said my brother. 'I'm in a hurry. I know what you want.'

'You think you know. But you don't know. You know nothing.'

'You want more booze. No stopping.'

'I'm talking to you now in a non-aggressive way. This is important. It is the best that I can do. I want you to understand something; sometimes I get impatient. It's like a disorder . . . I need you to stop the car NOW!'

He sneered. 'I know your disorder, Bruno. You can pick up your whiskey later.'

'Stop the fucking car!' I yelled, smashing my fists over and over into the dashboard. 'Pull the-fuck-over!'

'We're supposed to be at the hospital.'

While holding Fab's watch in my teeth, I tore the plastic bands from each side of the dial and spit them on the floorboard of the car. Then I threw the watch at the windshield.

'Pull over, motherfucker!'

'What's the problem now, Bruno?'

'Cockshit! I'll crush your eyeballs out your asshole.'

Watching me, my expression, he turned the station wagon into the store's parking lot and stopped. 'Look at you,' he said, shutting the engine off. 'Look what you're doing. Are you crazy? What's the matter?'

'Shut up!' I yelled again. Trembling. 'I need you to shut your fucking fuck face!'

He was scared, but he removed what remained of the damaged watch from the polished dashboard, saw it was still efficiently timing the ride, then hit the stop button to temporarily halt his elapsed time. 'Okay. Calm down,' he whispered. 'What now? What do we do now?'

I got out of the car, walked a step or two, then hunched down and began puking between Fab's car and a Volvo parked in the next slot.

Fabrizio came around the front of his wagon. 'Can I get you something for your stomach?'

I was still puking. 'Move away.'

'Why are you mad at me?'

'Don't talk. No speaking.'

He waited, watching me retch. When I was done, he spoke

again. 'Would a drink help? Do you want me to get you a bottle of something?'

'Yes. You can do that,' I said, still tasting the sourness in my mouth. 'Get me a pint of Ten High.'

'You're upset about Dad, aren't you?'

'I don't know.'

'I recommend that you talk about it.'

'Get me the bottle, Fabrizio. We can share ourselves fully some other time.'

Chapter Four

I HAD NEVER been to Cedars Medical Center. It was enormous, with levels and levels of parking. Montefiore in New York was small by comparison. This was a sickness mall. A gleaming cash register of a hospital.

Inside, through two sets of double-doors and long linoleum halls, the hospital was like every other hospital. The smell was the same. Fab was a quick, impatient walker, always staying busy, always running some compulsive mental contest. I kept up with him until the idea of seeing the old man and the odor of the place made my stomach ripple again.

When we passed a men's room, I stopped and called to Fabrizio to go ahead without me. He paused, shot me a backward glance, making a face that seemed to say that he didn't care what I did. He was satisfied that he'd gotten me there. Before he went on, he called out our father's room number over his shoulder.

Inside the first bathroom stall, I bolted myself in and sat down to take a piss. But I did not piss. I clenched my eyes closed as long as I could, breathing in and out.

I felt my heart slowing, so I blew my nose and lit a cigarette, then flushed the crapper.

The bathroom was not a main hospital crapper. It was a kind of employee john, so I hoped that I would have a few minutes of privacy.

I sat there for a while. Thinking. Letting myself relax. From time to time, I sipped at the pint bottle in my coat pocket. I lit more cigarettes.

There was no graffiti or writing on the blue walls of the stall and everything was clean and new-looking. When the bottle was gone, I counted the smoked butts floating in the toilet. There were four. Three of them had little brown streams drifting downward in the toilet water. They were grouped together and were about the same length, smoked the way I always smoked, to just above the filter.

The fourth was a nonconformist. Longer. I watched it bobbing alone. Then I stood up and directed my stream of piss on it. It failed to break. My stream wasn't strong enough. I was getting old.

The main door to the bathroom clicked open and I heard my brother's voice. 'Bruno?' he whispered.

'What?' I said back.

'You okay?'

'Yeah, okay.'

'What are you doing?'

'Go away, Fabrizio.'

'Are you coming?'

'In a few minutes.'

'But you're okay?'

'I'm preparing. I'm okay.'

'You've been smoking in here. In a hospital. There are rules about not smoking.'

'Fuck you, nurse.'

'Rules. That's all I'm saying.'

'How's the old man?'

'Still alive. His lungs are filled with fluid. He's not good.'

'You go on back. I'll be along.'

'When? . . . Mom wants to know. She wants to see you. We're all in the waiting room. What do I say?'

'I don't care what you say.'

'How soon are you coming?'

'When I'm done here.'

'What are you doing?'

'Go away.'

My sister Margaret was the first person I saw when I got to the waiting room. Maggie. Then my mother. Then Benny Roth, Maggie's husband.

Maggie jumped up and hugged me. My little sister. She was five years older than Fabrizio (Tommy) and seven years younger than me. She had new tits, done since I had seen her last. She hugged and kissed me, then made a face like I had an odor.

I hugged Mom. She smiled too. She seemed glad to see me. Benny Roth shook my hand.

I sat down and Mom told me in greater detail what I knew already. She had gone in to wake up the old man in the morning four days before and had been unable to get him to open his eyes. He was groggy and not making sense, so she called old Dr. Macklin, who had had my father immediately transported to the hospital by ambulance.

Macklin, my father's doctor for twenty-five years, to be sure about his diagnosis, had called in Dr. Helmut. Helmut was not really a complete expert and not 100% sure in these cases, so he had called in Dr. Stein. Stein was the final authority.

After two days of needles and fluid samples, monitors and many expensive tests that further traumatized my father's body, everybody agreed unanimously, without a doubt, Jonathan Dante would die.

I'd been in the ICU waiting room only a few minutes when a jittery, high-strung transvestite calling himself Copacabana made his own entrance. He was wearing black stretch pants and a fitted top that came to just below his rib cage.

Copa joined Dwight, a straight-looking college-type young guy who'd been watching TV. They sat on the couch across the room, opposite the one my mother, sister and Benny Roth sat on.

Cedars is only a few blocks from Hollywood, and it made sense that many emergency OD's and drive-by shooting casualties would show up there, instead of going to hospitals in L.A. that were further away. I didn't give a shit what misadventure had occurred to bring Copa and Dwight there, it just pissed me off to have to tolerate them. Copacabana was whacked on something that impelled his body to get up frequently and change the TV channel. When he wasn't talking, he'd suddenly lurch to his feet and hurry across the room. He would then look around defiantly at everybody, adjust his tank top or cinch up his tights, dial the set wildly in one direction, then back the other way. He seemed to prefer sitcom reruns. After he'd found a program, he'd return to the couch, laugh crazily at things that weren't funny, get bored quickly, then do the same thing again.

Copa's roommate and lover, Paris France, had eaten a bottle of Percoset and choked down several mouthfuls of drain cleaner because the day before, Copa had admitted he was in a new relationship. It was Dwight that discovered Paris France on the kitchen floor.

I was embarrassed by their conversation about the suicide attempt. My family knew that I knew about insanity and self-killing. They also all knew that, concealed under the sleeves of my shirt on my wrists, were six deep scars with stitch marks. Razor tracks. The recent sutures from the operation after my stomach mutilation with a steak knife were not yet healed. I hoped they didn't know about them.

But, as Dwight and Copa talked more about the details of Paris France's attempt, I could sense the eyes of my family on me. I realized then that Agnes must have filled them in.

We were allowed back in to my father's bedside after a final try to revive his kidneys had failed. We formed two groups: Mom and Maggie and Benny Roth would go first, then after they returned, Fab and I would be allowed in to say our last goodbye.

Loving Jonathan Dante had not been an easy thing for anyone to do. I was sure his intense pride would have prevented him from conceding to have anything other than a doctor or a priest at his deathbed. I didn't want to see him there, alone, his power gone, without hope. I didn't want to see him at all.

When Fab and I entered his room, I realized how unprepared I had been. My eyes confronted a blind, legless torso and my brain was unable to accept the input of my senses. I did not recognize the shriveled half-person that was now my father.

Diabetes had hacked off his toes, then his feet and legs, then caused complete blindness over the last five years. I knew these facts. I'd been told everything in phone calls. Now I was seeing.

I went to the bed and picked up one of the hands. The fingers were short and thick. Hammer handles. I recalled those fingers. I remembered once thinking Michelangelo must have had fingers and hands like these. My father's stubbed fists had fashioned priceless words that had spilled from his typewriter on to acres and piles of paper that had created an extraordinary river of honesty and pain that became Jonathan Dante's work. Dante novels. Now the river was dry. I bent my head and put one of the hands to my cheek, hoping to say something to this ghost. But no words came.

Instead, I could hear his breath, thick and congested, coming in gasps. I knew that he could not hear me, that his brave heart would stop soon, and he would die, never knowing I had stood there at all. Finally, before I could set the hand down, I heard myself say, 'I love you.' Saying the words, what I felt was something like sorrow, but it was not sorrow, it was far deeper. It was the emptiness of a hole that would never be filled.

Chapter Five

IN THE WAITING room we all sat, expecting the appearance of Dr. Stein. It had been decided by my mother to pull Jonathan Dante's tubes out and simply let him die. She needed Stein's permission.

Copacabana was furious with Dwight. Copa's lover, Paris, had left a suicide note and Dwight had been withholding it. Paris had been pronounced dead and only now had Dwight finally handed the note to Copacabana.

We sat on our couches across the room watching Copa read the message on the paper and go nuts. The note blamed him, and Copa was much too loaded to be blamed.

He jumped up and began cursing Dwight for taking Paris France's side even though Dwight had said nothing. Next to me, I could see that Fabrizio found the whole display intolerable. We were the serious grievers.

Finally, I asked Copa to please shut the fuck up. That we (my family and me) were in the room too. What I said made him crazy. He came at me, crying and spitting like a child in a tantrum. 'You can lick the shit off my dick after I fuck mommy up the ass,' is what he screamed in my face. Then, 'Leave me alone, you cocksucking little runt dyke!'

I got up without considering anything and hit him in the face. He went down suddenly when the blow caught him flush on the side of his cheek.

For a second he lay there holding his jaw, stunned. Then

quickly, stupidly, he got up and lunged at me again with insane eyes.

I hit him more, this time in the mouth and on the side of his head behind his ear. He fell hard against the linoleum and his skull made a thud as it collided with the polished surface.

There was blood on his shirt and face as he rushed me again, clawing and tearing at my hair and skin.

Now I was afraid he was on something like Sherm, that killed pain, or a form of speed. He might just keep coming at me.

I was angry. I wanted to fuck him up real good.

The next time he charged, I threw him down and hit him again and again in the nose and mouth until my own fist bled and ached.

Fab and Benny Roth pushed me off.

After it was over, my mother wouldn't let me stay in the waiting room. Maggie had called a hospital cop who insisted that I leave before I was detained. Dwight got Copa onto the couch and he looked like he'd be okay.

Because Fab was returning to Malibu to pick up my wife and bring her to the hospital, I decided to have him take me back there. They insisted that Fab leave immediately and take me along.

It cost ten dollars to get out of the hospital parking lot. Fab paid. On the way down La Cienega toward the freeway he was excited about the fight and wanted to talk about what had happened. I didn't.

I had a desperate need for silence. To be alone. I wanted to catch the next plane for New York or Texas, or be dropped off in the desert. I was shaking uncontrollably and unable to calm down. To subdue my rattling hands, I pinned them under my armpits. Then I demanded that he stop at the first liquor store.

Fabrizio ignored me. He was popping out strings of syllables like an out-of-tune car that won't stop running after the engine is turned off. On he went about my fight and then about a punchout of his own that he had with an ROTC guy two years before while on weekend maneuvers.

Something in Fabrizio's history had permitted him to conclude that anybody riding in his car must listen to what he was saying. Did I always react with violence? Did I have to fight a lot in jail and in my in-patient programs? Did the cops ever club me when I got arrested? Was it my experience that the majority of men turn queer behind bars?

I grabbed his arm and squeezed the bicep as hard as I could. People like him, I yelled, always got butt-fucked first in jail by brothers named Bubba, because people like him were self-righteous, dickless punks. Easy targets.

I was close to out-of-control again and he could sense it, so he pulled into the next liquor store parking lot.

My mind was still racing and crazy as I got out of the car. I sensed that my body might be giving out too. The nausea was back. There had been only four or five hours' sleep for the last few days. The feelings that I was having were too fast and too many. I hoped some drinks would push the head into relaxation and help the body not puke or die. I hoped this time I'd be able to calm down because, for months, whiskey had only been working irregularly.

I got my bottle and a carton of Marlboro Red and when I was back in the car I told my brother that I was sorry if I'd scared him. I said I was sick and messed up these days and that I didn't mean most of the things I did and that was why I kept getting locked up all the time. He made a face like he understood. Like I was a whacked out deranged fuck, but that it was okay.

We headed south again on La Cienega. 'You're really shaking bad,' he said.

'I know,' I said, cracking the bottle and taking several drinks from it. 'It should be okay in a minute or two.'

'Tell me why you punched that queer so many times. I thought you were going to kill him. Your eyes looked crazy. Do you always lose it like that when you get into a physical thing?'

'It started out that he was out of line. Then I lost it.'

'Did you know what you were doing?'

'I think so. I didn't care. Sometimes I don't care what happens at all.'

After another long slam on the jug, I passed it to Fab. I was sorry for what I had said to him and for grabbing him in anger and I was still not sure that I had been forgiven.

It surprised me when he accepted the bottle and had a hit, then passed it back. My shaking was going away.

'Right,' Fabrizio said, his tongue swamped with saliva from the stinging of the whiskey, 'You inherited Dad's meanness, that nasty temper.'

'Correct,' I said, 'the temperament, not his talent.'

We took the Coast Highway. Not talking. Every time I passed the jug to my brother, he obliged and took a hit. At the area of the Malibu Pier, I suggested that we stop at a restaurant to make a phone call and see if Jonathan Dante was dead. I knew the answer. Fabrizio pulled in without argument. The whiskey had loosened his cork.

Inside the restaurant, a section was closed, still being repaired from the last fire. We sat at the bar, looking out the bay window at the water and the surfers. It was hot for December. Seventy-five.

The pretty girl bartender wore a starched tuxedo blouse, buttoned to the top, and a bow tie. She called herself Wilson and her black lacy bra with its doily pattern was visible, as her tits pushed against the inside of the front of the shirt. Her hair was black, too, and her lipstick was red-red and she free-poured a reasonable glass.

Fab made the call about the old man. I would not. He went to the bathroom to use the pay phone, while Wilson poured me number two and I waited for what was coming.

When my brother came back and sat beside me, he was smiling. 'He won't quit,' he said.

'He's not dead?'

'Not better, but not dead. He's hanging on. No life support. Stein told Mom it's his heart. It refuses to stop. It's the only organ he has still functioning and it won't give out. He's like a miracle.'

Then Fab began to cry. The booze had been a lubricant for him to finally love our father without restraint.

He drank and wept. Half an hour later, he was out of control and in love with Wilson and talking philosophically about death. His American Express card was on the bar, so she kept pouring.

He wanted to impress her, so he described how much he loved his father and what an unsatisfied poet's life the old man had led. Of course, Wilson had never heard Jonathan Dante's name as a writer of anything. Nobody had, except people in the film business, and most of them were dead.

The Dante I was remembering was more prick, less poet. This bar reminded me of the time when I was twelve when my father had told me and my friends that he was taking me to a Dodger playoff game. Instead, he'd gotten drunk and staggered in the house long after the game had been over.

My brother began reciting lines to Wilson from a poem he'd memorized long ago. I sipped my glass and listened. The words sounded familiar, like something clumsy out of my father's early work, like a lyrical passage from one of his novels.

Then I realized, to my shock, that he was reciting my own work from twenty years before, printed originally in the Saint Monica's High School newspaper. I'd written it as an English assignment and had eventually edited it and had it published in a Museum Magazine years later in New York.

Hearing the recitation terrified and sickened me. I began grabbing his arm, but he wouldn't stop. It reminded me of what a fake I had been as a writer. Pretentious, unskilled, shameless.

I felt as if some drunken Italian uncle had stood me on a chair at a family gathering and loudly related the story of discovering me in a closet masturbating. I was lucky it wasn't a long poem.

I said, 'Where did you learn that?'

'The old man. He knew it by heart. He gave me the magazine.'

'Don't do that again.'

Fabrizio leaned over to Wilson. 'It was beautiful, wasn't it?' he said. 'A snapshot of a poem. Like haiku.'

Wilson smiled, knowing that not talking was one of her best features. Fab put his arm around my shoulder. His speech was slobbery. '. . . a poet's harp – syllables dipped in truth . . . he always said you had the gift . . . he loves you.'

The year I had written the poem in high school, I had gotten a letter from my father addressed to me with Italian stamps on the envelope. He had been in Rome, rewriting scenes from a gangster show. It was the only letter I'd ever gotten from Jonathan Dante. There had been no mention of the poem but I knew that was why he wrote to me. It was his acknowledgement.

I still had the letter. I kept it folded in the fly leaf of a book of Pirandello short stories.

Chapter Six

IT WAS SUNDOWN when Fabrizio and I arrived at the Point Dume house. I drove because Fab was very drunk. I was blasted, too, and tired as death. As I eased his big Country Squire wagon through the back gate to the carport, I could see that the place was dark and abandoned. It meant my father must still be alive.

I unloaded Fab and we made our way to the back door. He told me where to find the house key, and I remembered that it had always been kept on a bent nail under the gas meter box outside the back porch. Propping Fab up against the rail of the house, I groped in the darkness until my fingers touched the key.

Opening the back door, I heard a noise behind me. It was Rocco, old and friendless, his ribs bulging through his dirty, sagging coat.

There was something in the dog's mouth, but in the darkness, it was hard to make out what it was. I reached inside the house and flipped on the porch light. In the clear beam, I could see that it was an animal. Small, wet and lifeless. It stank too.

He was emitting a high-pitched moan to get my attention. I closed the back porch door and descended the steps to where he was standing at attention. As I did, he dropped the corpse at my feet so that I would be better able to acknowledge his prize.

The violated animal's carcass had a large crushed head and

a fat, little body with matted hair. It had rodent-like feet but its tail was too short to be of the genus *Rattus*. I assumed that it was a gopher because I remembered my father saying once that Rocco was good at catching gophers.

The dog had patiently stationed himself near the back door to present his trophy. Waiting for the sound of my father's voice.

But I wasn't Dante. I had no fondness for dogs. Although, for a moment, I felt bad for Rocco. But so what. I wasn't going to congratulate him on murdering a gopher.

We stood looking at each other. He continued humming his high-pitched falsetto and appearing tense. His whining stopped only when he took quick, short, deep breaths.

I could see that he wanted a reaction, for me to scoop up the rodent, then pat him on the head and say, 'goo-boy.'

I didn't. I turned and started back up the steps to the house. It was the wrong move and it pissed him off. The humming got suddenly louder until, when I didn't stop, it became a snarl. I was afraid. Filled with whiskey, but afraid. He might attack me. There was a story the old man told about Rocco biting the gas man after he'd mistakenly patted my sister on the head. I wanted no trouble.

What I did was stop, a compromise maneuver, halfway to the top of the steps. I had no skill at dealing with an angry dog. But he waited, too, studying me with intense concentration. It was a standoff.

Something my father had told me years before came to me. A statement of how he dealt with meeting new people. To define his own territory, my father would insult the other guy in the first five minutes of conversation. It made me wonder if Rocco might not be imitating the old man and doing the same thing.

When he didn't charge, I felt braver and decided to sit

down, even pulling my cigarettes from my jacket and lighting one up. His humming started again, but he didn't advance. The stench of the dead carcass seeped past the haze of my booze, its foulness hitting my stomach and lodging there like the ache from food poisoning.

Five minutes passed that way. Finally Fabrizio puked over the porch rail, a projectile stream that panicked Rocco. It caused the dog to snatch up the gopher and disappear into the night.

Once inside the house, I put on some coffee and steered my brother into the bathroom where he cleaned himself up by splashing water against the puke on his 'SC' sweatshirt and rubbing it in with a towel.

My body was exhausted. Too tired to telephone the hospital and hear bad news. My own confusion kept my mind numb, under control. Walking Fab into one of the guest rooms, I sat him down on the bed where he fell back, rolled into a fetal position, and immediately passed out.

In the kitchen, I poured myself a cup of coffee with four fingers of whiskey in the mug and pressed playback on the answering machine next to the phone. If there had been a change in the old man's condition, there would be a message.

I was curious what the people who knew my father and mother were saying, so I listened to each message, peeping again into my parents' lives for insights that had eluded me during my childhood. What were people's expressions of hope and distress? What emotions were they reciprocating? Why did other people like these odd creatures?

A dozen different calls had come in over several days and were being stored on the machine by my mother, Judith Joyce Dante. She was collecting them and I knew that she would answer each at the appropriate time. It was her way.

She'd respond in order, systematically, like she did every-thing.

There were upset friends from Northern California and Colorado, my mother's sister and her husband, two Italian cousins expressing drama and sorrow, neighbors showing concern, and a few calls from movie people.

One message in particular shocked me. It was from Phil Asner, a once famous TV producer-director and former poker buddy and friend of Jonathan Dante. His presentation of lamentation and alarm seemed completely genuine. I was surprised because I knew that he and Dante had not talked in years. My father's cruel tongue had destroyed the friendship. Dante had the terrible knack of uncovering another person's weak spot, then waiting for a vulnerable moment so he could crush that spot with an ax.

Asner and the old man had pitched a film script/director package together fifteen years before. It would have been Asner's first movie after a successful TV career. The deal had gotten funding but dissolved when the studio opted to do another project first. However, a close friendship had developed over time between the two men. Then, several years later, Dante sent his pal a manuscript of an unpublished novel he'd written that he thought had good film potential. Asner had been busy working and made the miscalculation of not getting back to my father quickly enough. Six weeks later, when Dante did get him on the phone, Phil said he thought the idea needed development, that he didn't see it as a film. Dante's reply had ended the relationship. He told Asner that the reason he'd never 'made it' in movies was because the sitcom format was the only way he could ever recognize clever writing. Phil's personal contribution to TV history, Dante had gone on, ranked on the list below the imbecile who had invented the laugh track. The two men never spoke again.

The last voice on the machine was my mother's. Dante was still holding death off on sheer self-will, without the aid of machine or drug. Why the old body wouldn't give up could not be explained by his doctors. My father, somehow, was reserving the extinguishing of life's last embers to his personal timetable. Dictating terms again. His pride was remarkable.

I decided to leave a message on the old man's behalf. I knew that my mother would pay more attention to a request from me if I were one of the voices on the answering machine. She'd have to. It would be a recorded message requiring a response. She'd take my name down and deal with me like she dealt with everything else on her 'to-do' list.

I pressed the 'memo' button and started talking. 'Hi Mom,' my message began. 'Bruno Dante here with something to say; when Pop's gone, I hope somebody will be taking care of Rocco. I know you've got a lot to deal with now, but I'm worried about the dog. He's bewildered and gaunt and fucked up. He's abandoned and half-dead. I know that Dad would want him looked after. Okay? Tommy (Fabrizio) is too occupied with his corporate financial mental shit and Maggie keeps herself hysterical running around kissing Benny Roth's ass but I think the dog should be a priority somewhere. That's my opinion. Thanks, Mom.'

Then I hit the stop button on the machine and took the last swig of my coffee.

Recovery had given me some coping skills. Hot showers sometimes induced sleep in me, so I decided to take one. I was smart enough to know that if I didn't rest soon, I'd get drunker, maybe find some wine, then black out and stick a butcher knife into my stomach.

I undressed in the bathroom and stepped into the shower and turned the water on as hot as I could take. I lathered up and washed my hair and even tried jerking off with the soap suds, but lost interest when my dick wouldn't stay hard.

Then I let the water run on me for a long time, while I leaned against the wall of the shower to steady myself. When I could feel my body loosening and my mind quiet, I got out. At ease. Feeling ready for sleep.

Because of the hot shower, my mind was gratefully omitting its persistent reruns of me coming out of blackouts with my cock going in and out of other men's assholes, and memories of me waking up in my bed, choking on the stench of my own diarrhea, infested by a bestial depression until I drank again. Being alive to face the terrors and pictures of those moments was what made my death more and more necessary. But for now, I was safe with my secrets. I could rest. I lay down on the bed in the empty room and let blackness swallow me.

Chapter Seven

IT WAS STILL dark when I opened my eyes again. Looking at the lighted digital clock on the nightstand, I could see that over three hours had passed. Down the hall, I heard the water in the shower running and I knew Fabrizio was awake too.

I dressed in the blackened bedroom, not wanting to see myself in the mirror, fumbling into my clothes. In the smogless, clear Malibu night, the light from a big, powerful full moon surprised me with its brightness and caused me to walk to the window.

Outside, I saw Rocco once again near the back porch steps. He was where I had left him hours before, still facing the door with the gopher body between his forelegs, waiting for the approval of a master who would never return.

After taking a piss, I made my way down the hall toward the kitchen. The door to my father's study was closed. I paused. Nobody ever entered except with the old man's permission. Swinging the door to the dark room open, I waited for his demons to leap on me. None did, so I hit the light switch and let the incandescent light from his desk lamp assault the walls.

The room was unchanged from the last time I'd entered it to talk with the old man – seven years before. The furniture was old, sturdy office stuff. Heavy dark oak and mahogany with fat, solid legs. Each piece had been picked from one of the used furniture stores on Western Avenue.

On the far wall above a bookcase was a large, grainy, old

framed photo of H.L. Mencken, his hair parted severely down the middle and his shirt collar heavily starched. The great iconoclast was scowling.

The books on the shelf behind his writing table were the important ones. The sacred stuff. Unlike the other novels in the room, they never moved, except to get reread. There was all of Knut Hamsun, all of Sherwood Anderson, all of Jack London. In Dante's house, only great literature, art, and great writers got talked about. Men of accomplishment, like himself. Men to be feared and reckoned with. Other discussions were unimportant.

The rest of the books in the room that weren't on shelves were in stacks on the floor. Most of them were by good writers, but Dante never actually read them. He was a skimmer, completely impatient, always unimpressed – he'd read a whole book that way – a few paragraphs at a time. He'd read the first sentence of each paragraph, then move on.

From the bookcase behind his writing table, I pulled down a copy of *Hunger* by Knut Hamsun. This book, my father used to say, caused him to become a writer. I held it in my hand and flipped through the old pages. Somewhere in the middle, I discovered a sheet of typing bond that had been folded in quarters. It looked to have been used as a bookmark. It was yellow from age at the top where it had been exposed to the air.

I unfolded the make-shift bookmark and immediately recognized the handwriting as my father's. But over and over, the signature written was Knut Hamsun. Knut Hamsun. Knut Hamsun. A paper was filled to the bottom of the page. The eccentricity jolted me because I'd done the same thing a hundred times, filling legal tablets with e. e. cummings' signatures. The old man and I had things in common after all.

I refolded the paper and stuck it in my pocket, then put the book away. Leaving the room, I flipped the wall switch and returned everything to darkness.

At around eight a.m., I sat on the back porch steps after more cups of coffee that were mostly scotch. I got an idea. Rocco was still guarding his rodent in the morning light when the thought fully formed; the dog had the right to say goodbye to Dante in the hospital. My father had been his master his whole life. Now his time had run out too. I was sorry for Rocco's situation. From now on, his life would only get worse.

I walked to where he sat on the grass with his stiff gopher. Kneeling, I tentatively petted his head once or twice. He didn't respond. I noticed that a few of the old dog's teeth were gone or broken, and he'd developed a bald spot near the tail where his short white hair had fallen out. Happy fleas and ticks had been rollicking unmolested there for a decade. This animal had no friends left and he didn't seem to want any. He reminded me of his master.

When I went back into the kitchen and told Fab that I had decided to bring Rocco to the hospital to say goodbye to Dante, he rejected the idea. No animals were allowed in his station wagon or the hospital. Fab's mood was ugly because of his hangover. He gave me another sermon, as if he himself had written the hospital rules regarding pets; although I knew he was making it all up. This only annoyed me and served to further strengthen my resolve.

When I suggested that Rocco's presence in the room might bring on a further change in the old man's condition, Fabrizio sneered at the absurdity of the idea. To him, it would have no effect whatever.

As he talked, I began to be disgusted at his condescending, officious tone, and his narrow, self-satisfied CPA mouth. I felt myself filled with spite for the situation, and for my brother.

To cut through the shit and get my way, I decided to shift to insanity. I screamed at him and called him a yuppy-cheezedick-fuck. Selfish pink-pussies like him were why people like me got suicidal and locked up and tied down in detox. Then I hurled my whiskey-filled coffee cup at the wall where it smashed into a thousand pieces. After that, Fab backed off and agreed to take Rocco with us to the hospital. He insisted, though, that the dog be kept in the back cargo area of his station wagon.

It wasn't easy for me to persuade the dog to do anything. Rocco was unresponsive to everybody except Dante himself and currently devoted only to his dead gopher. He had no collar or leash that I knew of, so I couldn't think of any way to get him to do what I wanted. I tried calling, whistling, and clapping, but nothing helped. When I attempted to pick him up bodily, he showed me his teeth.

Finally, I realized that the key to igniting his participation was the stinking gopher, so I returned to the house and brought back several hunks of cheddar cheese and, using them to distract him for a second, I made a quick grab and snatched the gopher up by the tail.

It turned out to be the right move. Once I had the carcass in my hand, he followed me around the lawn and down the walkway to the carport. Then, dangling the body a foot from his face, I led him to the rear gate of Fab's station wagon and he hopped right in. I put an extra pint of Jack and some hunks of cheese from the house in a plastic bag and stuffed them under the front seat for later.

With the dog in the cargo area, I closed the rear door of the wagon and rolled the tailgate window down all the way. I got in the passenger seat and honked the horn for Fab to come out. I made sure to keep the interior lights of the car out so that my fastidious brother would be unable to see the rotting body in Rocco's mouth.

When Fab got in, he was too hungover and too busy making calculations about timing the ride to the hospital to notice anything about Rocco's rat. Even his own bad mood was a secondary issue. What was critical, again, was our ETA to the IC unit.

We backed out of the carport, with Fab resetting the car's trip odometer and changing his digital watch to the 'seconds' mode. He looked back at Rocco, mumbled something, but kept his attention on the task at hand.

My brother hit the 'go' button on the stopwatch part of his 'G-Shock' chronometer and peeled out simultaneously. As we took off, I snuck a glance back at Rocco in the dark cargo area. All I could see was the top of his head. No gopher.

When the air current changed, I could smell the odor of decomposing flesh so, to counter it, I cranked down the passenger window, even though it was chilly. Fab wanted cold air for his nausea, so he kept his window down too.

My brother refused my offer of a drink or a cigarette. This run to the hospital was requiring all of his concentration.

We were wheeling it pretty good around the corners on Point Dume on our way to pick up the Coast Highway, when Fab put his hand to his nose. 'Bruno,' he said. 'What's that stink? Did that dog roll in something dead?'

I tried a diversion. 'Forget that. Who's feeding him now that the old man's not around? Not you?'

'Maybe Mom is,' he said. 'Not me.'

'Then whaddoyou care if the fucking dog stinks? He's not your dog.'

'He's filthy. I'm making a recommendation to Mom about Rocco. As you know, she's asked me to help her in dealing with these kinds of issues now.'

'I'm only a little terrorized by that idea. Want a drink?'

'No.'

'Like dogs?'

'No.'

'Then fuck you,' I said.

In just over seven minutes, we reached Cross Creek Road on the Coast Highway. Fabrizio couldn't be angry at me because he was preoccupied with his ETA. We were over a minute-and-a-half ahead of his personal best. He celebrated by gunning the big 460 Ford V8 as we approached the changing yellow light, and shouting 'yes!' when it turned to red and we blasted through anyway.

When I said I needed to stop and take a leak, the blood went out of his knuckles.

'Can't you wait, for God's sake?' he snarled, looking at his stopwatch. 'Do we have to do this every time?'

'Sorry,' I said. 'It's not a personal attack. Just pull over anywhere here, and I can piss by the side of the car.'

He hated me again.

A quarter mile up the highway, after we passed the Malibu Pier, there was a Colonel Sanders fast-food fried chicken store on the left. Fabrizio slowed down to pull in and chirped his stopwatch to the 'pause' position. Then he hung a left into the lot. As he jolted us into a parking space he announced, 'You've got sixty seconds, mister.'

I was part-way out the door before my brain remembered that I would be leaving my brother alone with the dog and the rotting gopher. I realized that the stink would become much stronger with the car not moving and no air circulation. I could already sense the odor. Reversing my actions, I swung my leg back in and closed the car door.

'Let's go,' I said.

'Where?' responded Fab.

'Away from here.' I made my tone sound hasty, anxious. 'I can't piss here.'

'What's the problem now, Bruno?'

'It's political. I can feel myself getting upset.'

'What's political about taking a piss?'

'Colonel Sanders.'

'What about Colonel Sanders? Since when do you give a crap about Colonel Sanders?'

'He's Iraqi. That's why you never see him talking in the TV ads anymore. I won't use a bathroom in a place of business that supports a genocidal dictatorship. Our boys died over there. American boys.'

'That's crap, Bruno! He's been dead for twenty years.'

'That's the assumption we've been made to swallow. At the treatment facility, I was shown photocopies of published documents that reveal a contrary view. He's now in hiding. They've discovered a link to Lee Harvey Oswald. The man whom we refer to as Colonel Sanders has used his fortune to help fund the research that eventually led to the development of the SCUD Missile.'

'Okay, Bruno, cut the shit!'

'I'm proud of my heritage and the fighting men who have defended our country. That's all. I won't piss here. I'm taking a stand. I'll wait until we get to the hospital.'

Fab didn't want to waste any more time arguing. He slammed the gearshift into 'R' and screeched backward out of the parking space. Then he chirped his stopwatch back to the 'on' position, pounded the gearshift lever back into 'D,' and squealed rubber across the Coast Highway. We were quickly up to the speed of the cars headed south.

The force of the car's acceleration had caused Rocco to tumble backwards in the cargo area a couple of times and bounce with a thud against the inside of the rear tailgate. I pushed myself up in the passenger seat so I could look in the back. Somehow the dog had managed to keep his jaws locked around the gopher cadaver with the car in motion. The clean Malibu air was once again blowing the stink away.

When we exited the Santa Monica Freeway at La Cienega, we were ahead of schedule, but Fabrizio wanted insurance. He flew past a guy on the right, and used a turn lane to get the jump on the cars at the next signal. When the light changed to green, he stomped on the gas pedal, and veered left around a parked car in order to cut off the other motorists that had the right of way. 'Yes!'

We lost a little time at the next two lights when they were off synchronized, but Fab didn't look concerned. He knew the route well enough to anticipate the delays and take them in his stride.

Since this was a good run, my brother's conviction was building. We were significantly ahead of his other faster times. With each vanishing block, he was more eager and confident, and so preoccupied that he forgot about the smell coming from the rear of his station wagon.

Our major challenge came at Beverly Boulevard and La Cienega. For some reason, there were seven or eight cars backed up in our left turn lane, controlled by a signal arrow. This made Fabrizio nervous.

When our lane finally did get its green arrow to go, only one vehicle made it through before the arrow turned yellow, then red almost immediately. The light was way off sync and out of whack. We were now buried at the end of the line.

What made it worse was that we were in a six-way intersection. Fab became very antsy, looking at his 'G-Shock' watch over and over, seeing his best run tick away down the shitter. He started pounding the wheel with his palms. He snarled out loud that the ninety-second light sequence would change at least six more times before we'd be able to make a left. There were now only two minutes left, and a block and a half still to go to beat his record.

Fab's lips formed the numbers of a countdown. Eighty-eight, eighty-seven, eighty-six. In front of us was a Jaguar convertible and behind us a yellow minivan. Then, unable to stop himself, he began blowing his horn, wildly motioning to the lady behind us driving the minivan to back up.

It took her a few seconds to understand and reverse her vehicle a few feet. Fab slammed our wagon into 'R' and skidded back, making solid contact with her bumper. Then, using the opening, he banged the station wagon's tranny into 'D' again and made a wild right turn across all lanes of traffic to the far right turn lane where there were no cars stopped. I knew what was coming. It was a favorite maneuver of New York cabbies. They do it all the time. When our light turned green, he edged his way forward into the middle of the intersection and waited for all the cars headed in our direction to go on through the intersection. Then, when the signal had changed to yellow and there was no more traffic coming, Fabrizio swung his illegal left from the far right traffic lane ... 'Yes!' he yelled, and punched the accelerator.

I heard Rocco groan as the force of the turn slid him and his gopher across the rear cargo area and bounced him off a wheel well.

We screeched west on Beverly Boulevard with forty-five seconds to go, while Fab continued to mouth his countdown. My kid brother was still confident of a record run.

With thirty seconds left, we wheeled into the automatic ticket-dispensing lane at Cedars' parking lot entrance. As it turned out, however, we were fucked. In front of us was a twenty-year-old mint condition Caddy driven by an elderly, fat man who had not pulled close enough to the ticket-giver machine to grab his stub.

I could see Fab's jaw muscles tighten in rage as the short-armed, old guy struggled, without success, through his open window to reach the machine. Finally, carefully, the old poop had to open his door and stretch to grab at the pink cardboard ticket.

Seven. Six. Five. Fabrizio slammed both hands on his horn and held it down. The noise of the horn was magnified by the low ceiling of the building.

Once, in St. Adrian's bar in New York City for the bribe of free drinks, a barmaid from Kentucky had mimicked to me the long, low mooing sound a steer makes when it is dying from a sledgehammer blow to the head. Fab's horn in the parking building sounded to me like that imitation.

It shook up the old guy in the Caddy, but he got himself together and pulled into the garage.

'Almost,' my brother snarled as we pulled up and he extracted his own ticket from the machine. 'Crap!'

'Let's *do* him, Fab,' I whispered. 'We're both half-Italian. Go ahead. I saw your pocket knife in the glove compartment. I'll watch your back. We'll follow the old asshole and cut his neck open and let Rocco lick the blood off the leather seats. The old fuck is probably here wasting Medicare money anyway. We'll be doing the government a service. Bet his fuckin' stupid ninety-year-old wife is wasting our tax dollars too, taking up a perfectly good bed in the ICU.'

'Shut up, Bruno. It was just a game.'

'Yeah. Right.'

Fab would not enter the hospital accompanied by our father's dog, so I had to agree to come back later and bring Rocco in by myself. I left him in the back of the dark station wagaon coveting the decomposing rat carcass.

Chapter Eight

MOM WAS THIRD generation Californian. Gold rush people. Her English ancestors arrived in America in 1635. They settled in Rumney, New Hampshire and were ship-builders and sea captains. Mom graduated from Stanford with honors three months prior to her sixteenth birthday. Now sixty-six, she still reads five books a week and talks to her best friend on the phone every day in textbook German. She'd also learned Italian and French from books and had become a published poet in San Francisco before she reached legal drinking age. And somewhere along the line, she'd formed an addiction to needlepoint.

As a little kid, I was sure that she knew everything about every subject, but I realized later that what she knew best was how never to disagree with the volcanic Jonathan Dante.

When Fab and I walked back into the waiting room, Mom was on the same couch, in the same spot where we'd left her ten hours before. Agnes and my sister Maggie were sitting on either side of her.

She'd been working on one of her English countryside cottage pattern needlepoints, which, for a long time, was the only pattern I thought needlepoint came in. Every room in the Point Dume house, except the kitchen, was filled with countryside English cottage pattern needlepoint pillows.

'I brought Rocco to see the old man,' I said to her, sitting down with Fab on a couch across from Maggie and Aggie.

'Maybe it'll help bring him back if he senses that his dog is in the room near him.'

'That wasn't a good idea, Bruno.'

'How's he doing?'

'Weaker. We're just here waiting. Are you drunk?'

'No.'

'But you've been drinking, haven't you?'

'I drink, Mom. You know that I drink.'

'The security people took that homo and his friend away. He was on drugs, you know.'

'I know.'

'Where are you keeping the dog?'

'In the car.'

'Just leave him there, Bruno. I don't want you involved in any more trouble. You're unstable. Agnes tells me that your problems are worse than ever. You've been back in that treatment center again – until just a few days ago.'

'Agnes has no right to puke up details about my fucking life without my fucking permission. Especially with my father dying in a fucking room down the fucking hall.'

'She says that they've diagnosed you now as a chronic manic-depressive. Your alcoholism is acute. You're suicidal. Is it true that you stabbed yourself in the stomach again?'

'I was in a blackout.'

'Why don't you stop, for Chrissake? Your father quit, didn't he?'

'I'm tapering off. Can we change the subject?'

'Agnes wants to divorce you, and I can't blame her. I don't think you're crazy, Bruno. For your father, for me, make an attempt to pull your life back on track before you wind up with AIDS or brain dead in a prison somewhere?'

'Is there a rule that no dogs are allowed in the hospital?'

'Of course there is. This is a hospital. Have some black coffee, dear. Clear your mind.'

When I got to the closed door of Dante's room, my fear rendered me unable to push it open. I was suddenly filled with the idea that he was already dead. I began to shake again. And sweat. Panicking.

Changing direction, I stumbled and walked as fast as I could down the corridor, making my way toward the cool darkness and safety of the garage, my head hammering.

After endless lefts and rights in the hallways, I got through the hospital's double doors to the parking lot and breathed in the gas fumes and fresh air. The coolness helped to steady me until I could find a quiet spot between two parked cars where I knelt down and slammed almost the whole pint of Jack that I had in my coat pocket. Again I breathed deep. In and out.

In a few minutes the head banging slowed enough for me to light a cigarette. Then I waited some more, hoping to feel the 'click' from the Jack. I lit a second cigarette and smoked that too. No 'click' happened, but gradually the edge was coming off.

I finished the bottle and scooted the empty under the dark green Benz I'd been leaning on. My shaking had stopped and I could stand, so I began searching in the garage for my brother's Country Squire where I'd left my spare pint of Jack Daniels and my father's dog.

I found the car quickly enough, but forgot that all the doors would be locked. I didn't want to return to the waiting room, so I sat on the back bumper trying to decide what to do. The realization came that anal Fabrizio must have a hide-a-key somewhere under the car.

I was right. Feeling around under the bumper, it took a

minute or two until my rattling fingers found a small metal, magnetized container with the spare keys in it.

Unlocking the passenger door, I looked through the back window and saw Rocco asleep with the dead lump of mangled hair and bones still between his legs.

He was awakened by the interior light that went on when I opened the car door. Rocco raised himself to the level of the top of the back seat, where I could see his wide, shark-shaped head and the gopher once more dangling from his mouth. It was then the impounded smell of the decomposing carcass hit me. My throat gagged shut from the intensity of the stink.

It was impossible to enter. I had to swing all the doors open and hold my breath long enough to climb in, start the engine, hit the air conditioner's fan button, then hop out to breathe again.

When the rancidness was mostly gone, I was able to sit inside. I located my spare bottle of Jack from under the seat and took some long pulls, waiting once more for my pulsating brain to get quiet. My thoughts were always the enemy. That, and the headaches.

I needed time by myself, to escape. To take Fab's wagon and get a hotel room and be alone. A quick check of my pockets told me I had sufficient money for several days. I'd find a porno movie and hang out and let the mouth of some stranger suck me off in the dark. I'd wait until Dante was buried deep, then go back to New York. Or somewhere. Wait until this shit was over. Just be anonymous. Not think. Not feel.

The booze had relaxed me enough to formulate that simple plan. First, I'd take Rocco into the hospital and deposit him at the old man's bedside. There was no harm in that. Benny Roth and Fabrizio could deal with the dog by themselves.

When my head pounding had decreased, I made my move. Getting Rocco out of the back of the wagon was pretty easy.

As before, he snarled and tried looking vicious, but I used the cheddar cheese hunks to distract him from the gopher, then snatched the dead fucker up by the tail.

Once I had the corpse away from the dog, I used the plastic supermarket bag to roll the body up, soaking it generously first with splashes of whiskey that countered its rankness. The result was satisfactory enough to make the thing less disgusting. Rocco dutifully followed me across the parking lot, then to the automobile entrance of the garage, always pressing his nose as close as possible to the bag containing the gopher.

Once inside the doors, we stopped at the first long corridor. I knew that, by having him with me, I would be breaking somebody's sanitation rule, or pissing somebody off, but I had had enough Jack in me not to give a shit.

When the coast was clear, we started down the hallway. I gripped the bag with both hands high on top of my butt, so Rocco would stay directly behind me, bobbing up and down after the out-of-reach carcass. Part-way down the second corridor, a night cleaning lady with a pinched, get-even-looking Filipino face, rolled her cart out of a patient's room and spotted us. She paused to make up her mind what to do. The look she hit me with required a defiant counter-glare. Luckily, she backed down and the dog and I continued to the end of the hall.

That was the only incident.

When we had made it as far as the closed door of the waiting room, I stopped to peek through the window. Dr. Macklin was sitting next to Mom in a private-looking discussion, while the rest of the family waited across the room on other couches. No one saw me. I was full of booze, but I knew that if they did, my escape plan would be screwed. Rocco and I kept moving to the door numbered 334. Jonathan Dante's room.

Having the dog with me this time gave me the courage to

not turn back. I got to the door and again waited. Finally, my body trembling, I thrust myself into the room.

At the bed, I again looked closely at my father's gaping mouth as it continued to force air into the hollow body. He seemed to be dissolving in front of me, his breaths more shallow and further and further apart. It was macabre.

I didn't want to stay. I wanted to leave the dog and close the door behind me and never come back. But I knew this would be my last chance, so I sat down on the chair next to the bed and took his cold palm in mine.

Oddly, he seemed to be repaying my grip, and I was startled by the strength of the pressure in his hand. Half of me dreaded the loss of my father, while the other half agonized over his suffering. I shut my eyes and spoke loud enough so that if God or some spirit were in the room, it could hear me. 'It's Bruno, Pop,' I said. 'I'm here . . . Just let go. For Jesus' sake, haven't you had enough?'

Somewhere in the caves of his mind, he must have felt the words because it was then that his breathing did stop. His grip on my hand continued for a few more seconds, but I knew he was done. I closed my eyes again because I couldn't bear to look.

After a long silence, I opened them and saw what I feared – his face going completely white. Translucent. The blood draining away from the front of his torso. Suddenly, Rocco was standing at the end of the bed. The dog knew. I was sure. For the first time, he'd stopped coveting the fucking gopher and his black eyes were looking from my father's lifeless face to mine, as if we knew an answer.

I let go of the hand and lowered Dante's wrinkled arm to rest on the bed covers. 'He's dead, Rocco,' I said. 'Pop's dead.' The bull terrier looked like a dirty white marine coming to attention, stiffening his body, listening to my words.

I would not be able to leave him alone with his dead master. Not now. I had no heart for it. In the confusion that was to come, there would be no one who would care for him. He was alone, too, like my father. He would have to come with me.

In the bathroom I found a white cloth hand towel I used to wrap up Rocco's dead rodent for transportation, so that the dog would follow me back out of the building to the car in the parking lot.

Opening the towel, my hands shaking again from the desperate need of a drink, I quickly put the stinking, little carcass in one corner and started folding it forward, the way a deli guy rolls up a sandwich in waxed paper.

I was about to leave with Rocco and the wrapped gopher as a lure, when a perversity grasped my brain. Across the room I recognized my wife's purse among the other handbags. I remembered that, in a wallet inside the purse, she kept several credit cards which still bore the raised letters that spelled out the name Mr. and Mrs. Bruno Dante. It was true that our marriage was over. That was what made it easy to convince myself that the one final accommodation – the use of a credit card from her purse – would be my last requirement of her as a wife. The reasoning for the act was simple, it was: 'fuck her.'

I opened the purse and sorted through the wallet with the see-through plastic sleeves where she kept all her credit cards, until I found a bright gold new VISA card among the others. I slipped it into the top pocket of my jacket.

As I returned the wallet to the handbag, another idea came to me. I should leave her an exchange, a memento, something for something. So into the purse, I dropped the towel containing Rocco's gopher. Then, with my index finger and thumb, I pulled a corner of the towel that forced the cloth to unravel dumping the smelly little body into the center of the bag. She and the PE teacher boyfriend could use it as a dildo.

*   *   *

Getting Rocco back out to Fabrizio's car without the gopher was not too difficult, since I had bypassed trying to get him to cooperate. I just carried him.

We traveled over halfway to the garage until he got too heavy. Then I took a clean sheet from a linen cart and fashioned it into a kind of harness around his neck. I was then able to pull and haul him the rest of the way into the garage.

I had never stolen anything from my brother before. I told myself that, as soon as the dog and I had a room someplace, I would call Fabrizio and let him know where to pick up the car.

Chapter Nine

L.A.'S WEATHER IN December is particularly nuts. The night had brought in more dry Santa Ana winds from the desert. The last few years, at Christmas time, people drive to the canyons to start fires hoping to burn the city down and see the disaster they've caused reported on the TV news that night.

As I left the hospital parking lot, great waves of black dust splashed tree branches and brittle shards of paper bags against the windshield of the Ford. I found Santa Monica Boulevard and headed west in search of an open liquor store, while Rocco dozed on the seat next to me. I wanted only to be numb and buying two bottles of Mogen David Mad Dog 20-20, would make sure I got there.

For hours after the liquor store, I glided along the near empty side streets and dark avenues with my head sorting and clicking through impulses and conclusions. The more gulps of Mad Dog I consumed, the more reasonable my thoughts became. I wanted only the aloneness and the humming of the tires.

By the end of the first bottle I was okay. I'd made it to sundown.

I got to Ocean Avenue and the beach and turned left to Venice Boulevard, then left again heading back toward downtown, continuing to let the world blow by in silence. From time to time, great gusts of hot air like giant cotton balls thumped the car in the darkness.

At Sepulveda, I went north again toward the mountains, until I crossed Pico and felt the tires hit what still remained of the shiny tracks from where the old trains had run. The rails popped up in places through the worn asphalt. The moonlight would hit the exposed metal for a few yards at a time, then the tracks would disappear back under the pavement, like the backs of eels gliding beneath the surface.

I drove more. Another ten miles. Fifteen. This time taking Olympic Boulevard downtown and back, passing 'Nickel Street,' City Hall and Chinatown.

Near Venice Boulevard and La Cienega was a mini-mart liquor store. Rocco was awake and antsy so I pulled into the parking lot assuming that he was hungry.

A young Mexican clerk behind the register watched me coming in. I speculated that he pegged me in the category of jerkoff or wino bum because his attitude was cocky and nasty when I asked where the dog food was. He spoke bad American, snarled something, and pointed to an aisle. As I walked away, at the end of his side of the long counter, I saw a woman sitting on a stool and almost hidden. His lady.

She was Asian and older than the kid. Vietnamese or Cambodian. And very sexy. Red-red lipstick and long black hair and a black doily see-through blouse. I saw her face fully as she glanced up from her magazine. Our eyes locked for a second. Hers were hard and beautiful. Freeway eyes. I knew that mine were empty. Then, when I looked too long, she turned away. I always looked too long.

In the canned goods aisle, I picked up a few tins of inexpensive dog food and was about to return to the counter, when I remembered that I had my wife's credit card tucked in my pants' pocket. I had the revelation that I could afford anything I wanted. I wasn't just another shit-sucking loser off the boulevard.

I put the cheap dog food cans down and walked back to the register and picked up a plastic shopping basket while the clerk's eyes followed me. He could tell that something was different as I started randomly choosing packages of potato chips and cheese puffs and throwing them into the basket.

I grabbed many cans of good dog food, and several bags of Fritos, and a new can opener – not the cheap-shit metal kind that hurts your fingers, but the $9.98 kind with the wide plastic handles. From there I moved on: a Genoa salami and ten kinds of frozen dinners and crackers and mayonnaise and salad dressing and a dozen brands of plastic-wrapped cold cuts were next.

Now I was having a shopping spree. Carried away by my good fortune and the Mad Dog 20-20, I returned to the counter to drop off my full plastic basket and pick up two more empties, piling my purchases next to the register.

The mean-spirited young storekeeper's full concentration was on me, but I didn't look up or stop to make eye contact.

As I proceeded to the hardware area, I felt his glare, while I loaded up a few packages of light bulbs, telephone cords, and plastic-wrapped flash lights. When I changed aisles, he moved too, along the back of the counter to where he could watch me. He was making it hard to concentrate. To retaliate, I decided to buy everything in the lane I was in. The cookie lane.

Oreos and Malomars went in and chocolate chips by the dozen. Bags and bags. Peanut butter and oatmeal and even twenty packages of coconut macaroons that I knew I'd never eat. I had a mission.

The Asian girl was watching now, looking from me to her boyfriend, to the growing mountain on the counter, fully involved in the exhibition. When he saw me smile at her, it was the last straw. He snapped, 'Okay majn. Bum. Jou ga monee to pay?'

I had him and I knew it. I was in no hurry. An American citizen in possession of a gold Visa card with a $5,000 limit doesn't have to rush. Purposely, I again glanced down the counter at the Asian girl to be sure I continued to hold her interest, then I smiled back at him. 'Right in my pocket, amigo!' I shot back.

'Shjo me,' he sneered.

'When I'm done, señor, you'll be the first to know. You need have no fear regarding full payment. American pesos for American products. Esta bien, amigo?'

I didn't wait for a reply. I wheeled around and made a beeline back to the cookie section, a little out of control from the effects of fortified wine and giddy at my own dialogue.

I swept two more shelves full of Ring Dings, Twinkies and cup-cakes into my baskets. Each one weighed thirty to forty pounds, minimum. I had to drag them the last ten feet to the counter.

When I began to dump the stuff on the counter he grabbed my arm. 'Hole it, majn,' he said. 'No more.' He leered at me.

I shook him off, leering back. I was bigger. A coward, but bigger.

'Jou put heem all bak, majn,' he said. 'Jou krazee. Jou done want disa chit! Jou too drunk to pay. Done make too much trubl in diza store or I goin' to fuk you up!'

My wife's Visa card slid easily from my pocket and skidded across the counter to him, the way a crap shooter throws a come-out seven. Leaning over, an inch from his face, I yelled, 'Ring it up, Ace. Ring it all up! And keep your fucking hands off me. As far as you're concerned I'm Donny-fuckin'-Trump.'

The kid couldn't decide whether to fight or take the plastic. Finally, reluctantly, he picked up the card and made a kind of spitting, throat-clearing noise, then phoned the Visa number to see if my card was stolen. He even repeated the process a second time to make sure. Then he wanted to double check my driver's license ID before adding up my purchases. I passed the license over with a smile. I had nothing to hide.

Totalling everything up took him twenty minutes. I watched the register tape get longer and longer until it touched the floor. While he did it, his sexy girlfriend went back to reading her magazine.

Then I remember making a cocky, stupid decision, one that always made me end up the same way. After the kid had added everything up, I told him to throw in two bottles of Mad Dog 20-20. Hitting the wine too hard is when I start having problems.

The bill came to $619.00 for everything. There were seven full cardboard boxes to be carried out to the car. I signed the credit card receipt with a flourish, big circles and loops, 'e.e. cummings.' The kid didn't notice.

As I was starting the motor, I took a last, long look back through the window at the girl. She was still on her stool at the end of the counter. Still reading her magazine. I knew she knew I was watching her, but she wouldn't look up. The complete ice queen.

Unscrewing the cap on the Mogen David, I toasted her holding my bottle up and taking a long, deep wallop. Her haughty attitude didn't matter. Mad Dog takes all the bumps out of the road.

I'd forgotten that the 'Dog' ride I was beginning was my first since getting out of the hospital. For me, a run on Mogen David was like starting to fuck a five-hundred-pound female gorilla. All choice is gone. The gorilla lets you know when it's time to quit. Sweet wine is like that.

Rocco was licking the cap, so I emptied the contents of the Milkbone box on to the blacktop in the parking lot and tore down the container and used it for a bowl. I poured a finger's width on the bottom and he licked it up.

I kept heading east on Venice Boulevard in the hot night wind, sipping wine and watching pieces of L.A. blow across the windshield. When I got to Western Avenue, I turned north and continued until I passed the Wiltern Theatre at Wilshire. I'd thought I was simply driving, cruising aimlessly as before; but when I saw the Wiltern, I knew I was only a few blocks from the Dante family's first house in L.A., outside Hancock Park on Van Ness. It was the first home the old man had purchased on income from Hollywood. Movie money. Blood money. I found the house and stopped in front.

Seeing the place again in the darkness swarmed my mind with thoughts of another life. It had been thirty years or more since I'd lived in the place.

The old man had bought it because his agent, Harry Goldstone, had felt it would be a good address for a successful Hollywood screen-writer and because it was close to Paramount. Harry negotiated a great deal on the place.

The house was paid for entirely by Dante's movie salary earnings. The old man had finally stopped turning down lucrative film assignments and had completely given up being a novelist. After years of writing straight fiction and nearly starving, it was an easy decision.

We moved to Malibu when I was still young, but I could vividly remember this house and his rages here. It was here that, day in and day out, he rewrote stacks of scripts and reworked scenes on shooting deadlines. Here he had begun to earn the big money. Success and rage stuck to every wall of the place like black jam.

In this house, I was to experience what happens when a passionate artist gives up what he loves and comes to detest himself. Here, I had witnessed my father's drunkenness and seen him treat those closest to him with contempt and bitterness, while he'd watched his paychecks get bigger and bigger.

And now, sitting in the station wagon, it was Christmas time thirty years later. Looking at the house, I realized how Jonathan Dante might have spent summer nights pacing the master bedroom balcony, a glass of scotch on the rail, raising his rough laborer's fists to the sky, and cursing himself and God for letting him piss away his talent for a Hollywood paycheck.

Chapter Ten

I DECIDED TO drive some more. Tour around L.A. I'd been hitting the Mad Dog pretty good, taking long pulls as I stopped at each traffic light. I rode through Hancock Park, Mid-Wilshire, then headed back toward West Hollywood. When I got to La Brea, I swung north again. My plan was no plan. Float. Drink.

More   and more

              my mind shut

                      down

                      behind the wine . . .

              until

                      I was conscious of just

                              sections of

       time.

              Bits   and

                                      pieces of

              grey awareness.

                              Then . . .

v-e-r-y-s-o-o-n

it was

                                              all

                                      completely

              dark.

At the corner of Santa Monica Boulevard, I stopped for the red. It was then that I saw them. Hustlers. Boys. In the deadness of my haze, I wanted to fuck them all, suck every dick in a frenzy.

A blond kid, about eighteen, in a red halter top and cutoff jeans waved at me from a stand-up pay phone. Seeing that I was watching, he grabbed his crotch and smiled.

I tried to pull the car to the side to talk to him, but my leg wasn't listening clearly to my head's motor instructions. Slow motion had inhabited my brain. I knew that my foot would eventually go from the brake to the gas pedal, but it was taking great concentration. When the light changed, I heard a horn honking angrily behind me.

While I was re-thinking the directions to make the gas pedal work, I realized that there was a young black guy at the passenger door holding up two fingers. 'Two blocks man,' he leered. 'Just ride me two blocks to Fountain. Okay?'

I nodded and spoke. 'Okay, sure, get in.' My foot went back on the gas and started working okay again. The black kid got in, but the asshole motorist behind me kept honking and Rocco, who seemed passed out and unable to move across the seat, refused to budge. I had to drag him by his legs to make room for the passenger.

Once he was in the wagon and I had pulled away from the light, the black kid's pitch changed. 'So, what are you into?' he asked. 'What's your thing?'

'Tonight it's sucking and fucking . . . and not thinking.'

'Your dog . . . is he dead?'

'He's a sleeper.' I pointed to the bottle between my legs.

Looking around, he noticed the cardboard boxes in the back seat filled with cans and bottles and dozens of bags of junk food and cookies. 'You're into candy and potato chips big time, right?'

'Right.'

'I lied,' he said half-smiling, half-leering, 'about the ride – I ain't lookin' for no ride.' He was tense. He acted as if he were high on 'rock' or some kind of speed. The smile was a cheat on his face.

'What did you have in mind?' I asked, concentrating on the road to make sure that I was still steering the car okay.

When I looked back, he had unzipped his fly and was working his hand up and down a long, limp black dick.

'Want to suck me off? – Fifty bucks.' He didn't wait for an answer. 'I suck you – that's fifty, too – want to fuck me, that's a hundred – half-and-half is one-fifty – that's the menu, baby.'

'Okay, good . . .' I said, lying, turned off, suspecting that what he was after was money for more 'rock,' not sex. Suddenly, I wanted to get him out of the car so that I could go back to the boy in the red halter top or pull over to the side and sleep . . .

He saw me losing interest. 'You like pussy, too?'

'A personal favorite.'

'Listen to what I'm tellin' you, I got me some sweet young white hole stayin' at my place – pretty, too – tight little pussy – she from New York . . . she love drinkin' too . . . she fifteen, no shit, I saw her ID – suck your dick till it fall off – do anything I tell her – just give her some of that mean red piss you been drinkin' and let her pet your dog – she love to watch herself in the mirror take it up the ass and suck dick – nasty bitch – you can have her for all night . . . wanna go . . . ?'

I hated his hustle. 'How much,' I asked, bored.

'All night, two-hundred,' he said, his brain speeding and out of control.

'Let's forget it.'

He was desperate and had no patience. 'Fuck, man – a

hundred, then – FUCK – I need the money – you lookin' at me – you know I need the money.'

'Twenty-five,' I said, sure it would get rid of him.

'Okay – deal – FUCK . . . you too drunk, baby – fucked up – how I know you got any money at all?'

We were at Sunset Boulevard and La Brea, half a mile from where I picked him up. I didn't want to drive any more. I needed to pull over and sleep. 'OK,' I said, removing a fistful of fives and tens from my pants' pocket. It was part of the cash from my last four unemployment checks. 'I'm rich, see?'

'Let's go to my place – it's just five minutes – you can fuck her all night – it's on Santa Monica, past Western – not so far – she take good care of your dick. First, you pay me the twenty-five.'

I bumped the big Ford against the curb when I stopped. 'Bring her back here,' I said. 'I'll wait for you. Twenty minutes.'

'She won't come out the house – you gotta go with me – she don't trust nobody.'

I took a ten-dollar bill from my pocket and handed it to him, then reached back and pulled three bags of Malomars and a couple of packages of the coconut chocolate chip cookies from the boxes and gave those to him too. 'Give her this stuff and the money,' I said. 'She'll come. And tell her that Bruno said Merry Christmas.'

'Bruno? – bitch want money, Bruno – not no cookies.'

'Bring her back here. I'll give you fifty more if you bring her here to me.'

'You fucked up, Bruno – you crazy – you look crazy – been suckin' on that mean wine too long – don't be sendin' me to run down no pussy and not be here when I come back.' I handed him another five. 'I'll be here. What's her name?'

'Amy.'

'Okay. What's your name?'

'Call me McBeth, like the play.'

'Right,' I said.

A long time later, I woke up with Rocco barking and someone at my driver's window. A girl. Young, fifteen or sixteen. She wasn't pretty and she was very skinny, but she was smiling. I smiled back.

As my mind cleared, I saw McBeth at the other door, motioning me to let him in, so I popped the button. Rocco was snarling at him and he was afraid to get in. I held the dog by the collar.

'Sorry, Bruno, it take too long finding da ho – two hours.' By my expression, he could see that I wasn't impressed with her. 'Yeah, I know, she skinny as shit and she got a horse face, but she fuck you till you beg to get yo dick back and she smart too – whacchaamatta you dog, man – he like me before.'

'He was asleep before.' I hefted Rocco onto the floor of the back seat. He didn't resist and curled up. They got in.

When Amy talked, it was with an acute stutter. 'Is th-th-that animal va-va-vicious,' she asked.

'Is McBeth?'

'A pa-pa-putz, a ba-bad business man but na-na-not va-vicious.'

'You'll have to take your chances,' I said.

She smiled again. 'I la-la-like Ma-ma-malomar ca-ca-cookies.'

At McBeth's suggestion, I headed the Ford west on Sunset to Laurel Canyon, then north up into the hills. Looking over at Amy, I could see that she weighed under ninety pounds. A body of a child's. Her Hollywood-hooker costume of black high-heeled boots and thigh-high tights and a halter top made her look like a pre-teen playing dress up. Her tits were two knuckle-sized protrusions in the elastic top. A mile up the canyon, McBeth directed me to pull in behind the parking lot of the Country Store Market, so we'd be in darkness and out of view of the street. I did what he requested, and parked the car.

'Give the girl some wine – she love to get stupid – she love the shit,' he suggested. I took a long pull at the jug and passed it to Amy. He was right. She hammered at it for half a minute with long, savage swigs.

'Fuck,' I said, 'you are a drinker.'

'I ca-ca-ca-can pa-party,' she said back. Then she opened a purse that was crammed full of unwrapped Malomars, removed one and took a big bite.

I began to laugh from somewhere deep in my guts. Being with her and McBeth and my father's old bull terrier in a deserted parking lot in the Hollywood Hills in the Santa Ana wind, eating cookies and drinking Mad Dog struck me funny. It was like listening from outside my head. I passed McBeth the bottle and asked him if he wanted a hit.

He pushed it back. 'I want my money, man. Fifty bucks. We doin' binnes. You gonna fuck this ho? Yes or no?'

'I'm not sure,' I said, still laughing, heavily under the numbness of Mad Dog wine, indifferent to whether I got fucked or not. To make McBeth happy, I started pulling clumps of wadded-up bills from my pants' pocket and setting them on the seat for sorting. Amy took this as a cue, and bounced over Rocco into the cargo area in the back of the wagon, a Malomar in each hand. Half a minute later, she had managed to get her clothes off without having to set either of the cookies down. She was bony and pale and without embarrassment. Like a ten-year-old boy.

I was having trouble separating the money and watching her antics. To me, everything she did was funny. She reached back over the seat and began petting and feeding Rocco part of her Malomar, her narrow ass jutting into the air. That was funny too.

McBeth was quick. With one hand on the door knob, he scooped up and grabbed all the bills that he could, then jumped from the car and ran. When I looked over, he was gone. All I could hear were his footsteps. That was funny too. I yelled, 'McBeth, you thieving nigger fuck, take her too … Don't leave her here.'

Outside in the blackness, the footsteps came back to the rear of the car by the cargo door. 'Okay homie,' I heard him yell. 'You right. Fair is fair.' Then the tailgate door of the wagon popped open and he was inside next to Amy.

They grappled, but though she attempted to stop him, he was too strong and too fast, and he snatched up all her clothes and her purse, jumped out, slamming the tailgate door closed again. 'Now she all yours, white boy-crazy motherfucker,' he yelled. 'You so smart, Bruno, you figure this out. I'm done with both you now. Fuck you!'

I struggled out of the car, but he was gone into the hot night wind with my money and her stuff. It didn't matter. None of it mattered. The wine had done its job.

In the dome light from the car's interior, she looked bewildered, her thin arms and legs crossed across her pale torso. Like the boat people. Naked and luckless. Removing my jacket, I handed it back to her. Then I needed a few deep pulls at the jug – not to consider the situation, but because there wasn't anything else left to do.

We were a long time like that. Her in the back and me behind the wheel. I lit a cigarette. Then another. I could see her eyes studying me, expressionlessly, in the rearview mirror.

Finally, self-consciously, I smiled at her. It took a few seconds, but then she smiled too. I reached back and passed her the jug of Mad Dog and a fresh bag of Malomars. I figured, fuck it!

When I woke up, I was sweating. The pains above each eye were not synchronized. One stabbed, the other jabbed. I was being punched by different-sized staplers at half-second intervals. Someone was near me – above my head, breathing hard. Panting. I remembered Rocco.

I had been sleeping on something hard and gravelly. When I squinted my eyes, it was against airless intense sunlight and suffocating heat. I realized then where I was – the rear storage area of my brother Fabrizio's Ford Country Squire Station Wagon.

I had no idea where it was parked, but I knew that this wasn't jail. Looking further, I could see mounds of groceries all around me on the floor of the car. Food everywhere. Opened luncheon meat packages and piles of spilled corn flakes. Slices of bread and ruptured cookie boxes stewing in scattered soap powder. My pillow was an open bag of Fritos chips. Crumbs of the stuff clung to my hair. I peeled something sticky off my sweating chest. It was a section of crushed Malomar cookie, chocolate and marshmallow stuck to my skin.

Next to me was the skinny body of a boy without a dick – segments of the memory of the night before were coming back in grey flashes – Angie? – Edith? – Amy!

The immediate problem was the brutal heat and sunlight. With effort, I raised my head and looked backward above the window line and out the glowing, flat rear glass of the wagon. We appeared to be parked in a parking structure. The back of the car was engulfed by the angle of the brutal sun. The front was not. It looked much cooler up front.

Fab's wagon had power windows but the journey and effort to travel to the ignition switch next to the steering column was out of the question. It might be possible to make it to a shaded area in the rear seat but I was still incapable of attempting anything. My body wouldn't obey. I settled for wetting my raw throat with several swigs from the bottom of the Mad Dog bottle. It helped.

Gradually, I became aware of the sounds of car doors opening and closing. Footsteps. Voices. Amy's bony knee was resting in my crotch. Her body was sweating too. Naked. Shining in the heat.

When I moved her knee off my balls, her eyes opened and she smiled. I was forming a thought to make a sound to talk, when a security parking attendant guy in a uniform and white shirt with patches began banging on the hood of the station wagon. 'Hey,' he yelped – he had epaulets like the cops on the Garden State Parkway – 'You are directed to move this vehicle immediately. Impeding access to an entrance is a violation.'

Rocco charged the glass and snarled until the dickhead backed off. I covered my genitals with my free hand, leaned forward above the seat, and waved and nodded YES up and down to make him go away.

Then I tried looking through the back window again, squinting past the pitiless glare to see what was making the guard guy so aggressive. The rear of the wagon was a few feet from a door. The lettering on the door read, 'Cedars Hospital. Morgue Entrance.'

The car had a quarter of a tank of gas left when we headed west on Sunset out of Hollywood. It was the wrong direction to buy something to cure my headache, but I wasn't thinking good yet.

Driving slow, I slammed the last of a pint of Ten High and felt nothing. Amy sat quietly against the passenger door, naked except for my green army jacket, which she wore unzipped and wide open. She was eating handfuls of chocolate chip cookies, feeding some to Rocco. I could tell that she avoided conversation because of her stutter. That was okay with me.

She found a brush in the glove compartment and began to rake it through her hair, using Fab's sun visor mirror, humming, unphased by the prospect of a new day. Then she did talk: 'You ra-rich, Bruno ba-baby?' she said.

I wanted no conversation. 'Just Bruno, no baby,' I said back.

'I wa-would la-la-like you to ba-b-b-buh-buy me a Ka-ka-kup of ka-ka-coffee and pa-pa-pay meee for la-la-la-luhhhhlast na-night. Is tha-tha-there a pa-pa-potential of tha-that?'

'Maybe,' I said, struggling self-consciously to get my rattling fist into my pants' pocket, 'I'll see.' Then I remembered McBeth sweeping my wadded-up bills off the seat and running away.

I checked the other pocket, the left one, where I usually kept the bigger bills. (That was because, sometimes in bars, I would forget that I had my money in the left side, too, and I could trick my mind and not spend that pocket.) I felt a bulge and knew I was okay, surprised that she hadn't gone through my pockets and ripped me off while I was asleep. 'Looks like we're in luck,' I said, patting the pocket. 'It's pay day.'

She saw my expression. 'Da-da-da-did you tha-think I ta-ta-tahhhh took ya-your mah-mah-money? La-la-like Mmmm-mmmmaaaack-Beth?'

'I wasn't sure.'

'I'm a ka-ka-cock sa-sucker fa-for ma-money, na-not a tha-thief, tha-there is a da-da-distinction.' She slid her hand between her thighs and thrust a wet, smelly finger under my nose. 'Pa-pa-pay me now,' she demanded. 'I uh-uh-earned it.'

'Jesus, how much?' I said, reacting with nausea to the smell.

'Ta-ta-twenty fa-fa-five. I ba-ba been ga-getting fa-fifty but sa-since la-Lady MamaMc-ba-Beth ta-took ya-you off la-la-last na-night all ya-you na-need to pa-pay is ta-ta-ta-twenty-fa-five.'

I handed her my folded money, unable to peel any off because of my shaking. 'Take fifty,' I said, my head hammering.

She peeled off the bill and handed the money back. 'Tha-thanks,' she said wearing a big smile, 'fa-fa for the gra-gra-gra-gra-grat-tuuuu . . . the tip.'

'Easy for you to say.'

'Wa-want me ta-ta-to ga-give ya-you ha-ha-ha-ha-head ra-right here in the ka-car wha-while ya-you da-drive? I na-na-know I ka-kan ma-make you ka-come? Ya-ya you'll fa-feel ba-better.'

I looked at her unattractive naked body. No tits, only round, little pink nipples protruding from her rib cage. No hips, and the ass of an eight-year-old Little League right fielder. As a hooker, her only appeal was her sense of humor. I shook my head no. 'What I need,' I said, 'is aspirin. And something for my stomach and more wine. A lot more.'

'Ya-you're sa-sick, Ba-Bruno ba-baby. Ga-ga-go home and get some rest.'

'The wine and the other stuff will fix me.'

'Ya-ya-you la-la-love tha-that wa-wine, da-don't you?'

My head was screaming loudly and needed to be shut off. Pure hate toxin had started pumping into my brain like the ocean gushing through the crushed hull of a sinking ship. That was the problem. More wine was the only way to numb it. There was no rush, no pleasure, only oblivion and the need for more. Sometimes a Mad Dog run could last two or three days, sometimes weeks. When you're fucking the female gorilla, it's not you that decides when it's time to stop.

Now, my mind out of THE DOG, self-judgement stabbed at me and ripped at my guts until it would be impossible for me to exist in my thoughts. Without the wine, my head remembered only evil . . . A pimp junkie had stolen my money. I had allowed myself to get fucked by an absurd, handicapped child. My cowardice in leaving my family at the hospital the night before and not facing my father's death was completely selfish and without conscience. I'd stolen my brother Fabrizio's car. I was a degenerate, with an insatiable capacity for perversion. Incapable of change. I could do anything except not drink.

My head was too loud. Had Amy not been in the car with me, had I been alone at that moment, I might have aimed the front fenders of the station wagon into the path of an oncoming bus. Anything to silence the noise. She said that I loved wine, what I said back was, 'It takes the bumps out of the road.'

'Fa-find a sa-sa-seven-eleven st-st-store. uh-uh-uh-I'll ga-go in and ga-get ya-your ma-ma-medication. Ba-but fa-first pa-pull over sa-so ya-your da-dog ka-kan ta-take a da-da-da-dump.'

I looked at Rocco. She was right.

After you take Sunset west a while, Hollywood ends abruptly, crashing into Beverly Hills. Concrete sidewalks and glass office buildings suddenly recast themselves into estates with manicured front yards.

Hedges and bushes are sculpted into frightening animal shapes of big birds and seven-foot-high long-necked geese. Here and there, alien-looking gardeners pull lawn mowers and yard tools out of thirty-thousand-dollar, four-wheel-drive utility trucks. These are the only visible humans around, except for the scattered joggers who bounce along the street wearing earphones, trudging through the Beverly Hills pastures like creeping cars on a freeway.

I made a left to get off of Sunset, then pulled down on a side street to a medium-sized mansion with a big front lawn. The grass strip between the street and the sidewalk was twenty feet wide, so that my father's dog wouldn't be shitting on private property. Amy wanted to walk Rocco, so I stayed in the car, smoking and sipping from the last of my wine and attempting to not panic.

Rocco, leashless, crapped near the car on the green, matted grass, while two runners, a middle-aged couple, bounced past towing a handsome red-haired Retriever on a rope. I watched them coming up the street wearing headphones with matching jogging ensembles.

I'd forgotten that Jonathan Dante's old dog still had a killer instinct. My headache and the stupidness from the wine had distorted my reasoning, and Rocco looked tired and beaten, with half his teeth missing, dragging a bad rear leg as he walked. He seemed a threat to no one. But he was still a Bull Terrier.

He managed a sudden lunge to the right as the group of runners passed, grabbing the Retriever securely by the throat.

Amy stood, scared shitless and naked with my unzipped army coat wrapped around her tiny body, unable to move.

Then the lady jogger panicked and let go of her dog's leash, and the animals worked their way to the middle of the street with cars screeching to a halt. Rocco's jaws remained fastened in a death grip on the other animal's neck.

I knew that he would soon kill the Retriever. I could think of only one maneuver to separate the dogs: once, years before in New York in Central Park, to impress a girl poet before a first date, I'd grabbed the rear legs of her Bulldog, Winston, when he'd set himself in combat with a spaniel. By accident, I managed to dangle the dog upright by his back legs, holding them apart, until the other owner got his animal to safety. That night, with the help of a bottle of tequila, I got my dick sucked by Winston's owner.

I had to try it again. As quickly as I could, I got out of Fabrizio's station wagon and made my way to the scene of the action. Already, the loss of blood from the Retriever had transformed Rocco's white hair to a dirty, soaked, red-brown paste. While the husband jogger regained a hold on his dog's leash and pulled in one direction, I managed to grab Rocco by the back legs and heft him high off the blacktopped street, hoping he'd drop the Retriever. It didn't work. The fucker refused to release his deathgrip on the other dog's throat. Then, while his body was still in mid-air, I tried twisting him like a wet rag. It hurt Rocco and made him wince and yowl, but still he wouldn't let go. The other animal's blood was on my face and clothes. More spectators gathered, terrorized by the sight of the white shark-shaped dog, intent on murdering the defenseless Retriever. Amy did her best to fade back into the crowd and keep my army coat closed.

Everybody was on the wounded dog's side, me included. My skull throbbed and I felt myself on the verge of puking, starting to pass out. I was getting used to having him around, but at that moment, I hated the dog too.

Finally, panicked, I did the only thing that I could think of doing – I bit down hard on Rocco's ear, deeply, until I tasted blood. It shocked him, and he yelped loudly and released his prey. The man jogger was then able to pull his mauled pet to safety.

I sat on the curb, sick and exhausted, restraining Rocco with both of my arms around his chest. The other dog, out of danger but in shock, had broken loose and fled down the street in an act of self-preservation. In the distance, I watched his owners chasing him around a corner.

It was time to take Rocco and go, but I was too nauseous

to move. I assumed that the Retriever's jogger-owners would be back eventually to have a discussion about legal matters and vet bills. In Beverly Hills, potential litigation rarely goes uninvestigated. And I was pretty sure that somebody had called the police.

The gathered spectators, gardeners, a nanny, a few people that looked like residents, and the stopped motorists, were all leaving. I looked around for Amy and spotted her down the block getting into the back seat of my brother's car. A Mercedes convertible had pulled in while the dogs were blocking the street during the fight, and it was now parked in front of the wagon.

In a few minutes, I was okay enough to attempt to load Rocco into the car. Getting up, I hauled him along the street toward the passenger side of the station wagon, using my belt as a leash. He resisted all the way, probably hoping for a rematch with the beaten Retriever.

When we got near the wagon, a man wearing a cowboy hat and a business suit stood up from the Benz and imposed himself between me and the car. 'I hope you're not planning on leaving,' he said. 'There's unfinished business here to attend to.' His accent was mid-western, Chicago. He wasn't a cowboy, but he did wear boots and he was a full head taller than me and fifty pounds fatter.

'My dog is hurt,' I said back, lying. 'He needs a vet.' I could now see that he had positioned his car at an angle with his rear bumper against the front bumper of my car, intentionally blocking us in. There was a cable TV truck behind the station wagon so we were jammed in tightly unless he moved his car.

'Your pink-eyed monster tore the crap out of that Retriever. His injuries looked serious. We're staying put until the owners of the dog come back and decide what they want to do.'

He was too big to deal with head-on, so I walked around him, with Rocco in tow, motioning to Amy to open the car door. Then I scuffled the dog on board the back seat with her.

When I got to the driver's door, a safe distance from the cowboy, I yelled, 'I'm leaving. Move your fucking car now and don't fuck with me!' Then I got in and pressed the lock button down. He sneered his disdain, then walked to his convertible and reached in through the passenger window, pulling out a car phone on a long cord. Then he looked at me smugly and began dialing.

I figured that I had nothing left to lose, so I started the car and flipped the gearshift lever into 'D' drive range and floored it. The force of the torque from the 460 motor easily crushed the right rear tire of his convertible against the curb and I heard it pop like a loud balloon. Panicked, and waving his arms for me to stop, the guy saw the rear end of his Benz slide over the curb and come to rest on the grass, three feet in off the street.

I was still somewhat sandwiched in, but I had more room to maneuver now, so I banged the wagon into reverse and skidded back a couple of feet. My head felt relaxed and pleased, as I slapped the tranny back into 'D' and slammed it hard again into the back of the convertible. This time, his trunk buckled and his car got pushed another foot or two forward. He wisely stood back, out of the path of my brother's lurching, skidding station wagon.

After my third pass, another of his tires popped, but Amy was screaming and trying to get out of the car, so I stopped to see if I had enough room to maneuver the wagon back out into the street. I did. It was okay to pull away.

I knew that there was damage, but everything in the station wagon seemed to be working good and the motor was running as strong as ever. When we were down Sunset a few blocks into Hollywood, I looked back at Amy and the dog. 'Sorry,' I said, 'I guess I'm having a bad day.'

Chapter Eleven

I CONTINUED DRIVING east away from Beverly Hills, until we got to Western Avenue, then I turned south. It was still morning rush hour and the hot wind blew dust and palm branches and garbage around the streets. Amy was sullen and crouched against the rear door. Her feet were pulled up under my army coat and the only part of her body visible was her head. The dog was exhausted and moaning with each breath and noiselessly farting. Lethally. Cookie-wine farts.

I kept the windows down as we passed the nude mud-wrestling place and the porno shops, then crossed Santa Monica Boulevard. She hadn't talked at all. Finally, I said, 'Where am I taking you? Where do I drop you off?'

She didn't answer.

'Amy,' I said, 'my head's coming off. Talk to me or get the fuck out of the car.'

'Pa-pa-pull over at the na-next corner, ba-by, that store,' she said. 'I'll ga-get out tha-tha-tha-there.'

It was a mini-mart liquor store. I turned in and parked in a lined spot away from the entrance, then shut off the motor.

She glared at me. 'Wha-what you da-did ba-back there wa-was insane. It ska-scared the pa-pa-piss uh-out of ma-ma-ma-me.'

'I said I was sorry. I have no tolerance for self-righteousness.'

Then I had another thought. 'And I hate people who wear cowboy hats.'

Amy got out of the car and came around to my driver's door. She was smiling, saying goodbye. 'Wa-want ma-me to ga-get ya-ya-ya-ya-you sssssomething for ya-your sta-sta-stomach before I ga-go?'

I couldn't turn her down because I didn't want to get out of the car unless I had to. With difficulty, I reached a shaking hand into my left pants pocket and worked a fistful of bills up into the light.

She was impatient and snatched the money. 'La-let me da-do that,' she whispered, 'ya-you're a fa-fa-fa-fuckin' ka-case.'

Quickly, she flattened the bills out, counted them, then gave me a total. I had two hundred and seventy dollars in twenties and tens, the last of my cash from New York, not counting the credit card. She handed the money back. 'Wha-what do ya-you wa-want from inside?'

'More wine,' I said, 'Mogen David,' handing her a twenty. 'Two bottles, and aspirin. And Pepto for the stomach.'

'Ya-you think ya-you've ga-got a big da-dick, da-don't ya-you? Sometimes ya-you act la-like you're a ba-ba-big sha-shot?'

'I do?'

'Ya-you think ya-your da-dick is ba-ba-bigger than Ta-Tom Sa-Sa-Sellnock's?'

'Who's Tom Sellnock?'

She smiled again. 'Da-da-don't worry Ba-Bruno, I na-knew you wa-were wha-wha-whacked-out and ca-crazy and wha-wha-wha-when I fa-first sa-saw ya-you. Ya-you have ca-crazy eyes.'

Hers were big. Light brown. They softened her face. 'Wa-want ma-ma-me to sta-stay with ya-you today? Ha-ha-hang out? Wa-wa-we'll ga-ga-get the wa-wine and ga-go to ya-your pa-pa-place.'

'I don't have a place. I've only been back in L.A. for two days.'

'Fa-from where?'

'New York. New York City.'

I wa-was tha-there wa-once. Ah-I la-liked it.'

'My father died at Cedars last night. I was born here.'

'La-let's ga-get a ra-room. A mah-mah-mah-motel. Ya-you've ga-got money.'

'How much will it cost for you.'

'Ah-ah-I'm ma-moving ta-ta-today and picking up ma-my st-stuff from fa-fa-fuckin' Ma-Ma-MC-Ba-Beth's ah-ah-apartment. Tha-tha-that's it. I pa-promise. Ha-he's ta-two blocks fa-fa-fa-from ha-here.'

We got one of the bottles of wine free because Amy knew the day manager behind the counter. We continued down Western Avenue to Romaine and turned east. After a block, we pulled over in front of a pre-Hollywood Twenties Craftsman House with stone pillars supporting the porch. It had heavy concrete steps and was set far back off the street, falling apart. Amy instructed, 'Ta-take off your sh-sha-shirt and ga-give it to ma-me.' I did and she slipped the army jacket off her shoulders and pulled my buttoned shirt over her little body. When she stood on the sidewalk it came to just above her knees. Shoeless, she tiptoed up the walkway to the front door and let herself in the front door with a hide-a-key from behind a planter.

The heat made me shiver and I took a blast of the Mad Dog. I felt it go down and the bolt of cold relief exploded within me. I knew the throbbing would be relieved soon. So would the thinking.

While she was gone, I tried smoking a cigarette, but it made me retch, so I ate aspirin and had another drink and listened to the news on the radio. Rocco was asleep and motionless on the floor, yelping in his dreams. The news-guy said there were shootings in a beach city close by, and an automatic weapon had ended a dispute over a Christmas gift certificate at a shopping mall. It made me hope that Amy's noise in the house wasn't waking McBeth, who might be asleep in a bed next to a crack dealer named Bubba, with an unfavorable disposition toward honkies.

I looked up when I heard the screen door on the porch quietly slap shut. Amy tiptoed down the concrete steps carrying two large supermarket bags filled with clothes. She got to the car and set them on the hood, then leaned in through the window, 'I've ga-got wa-one ma-more thing to da-do,' she whispered, jingling a set of car keys and pointing to a Toyota convertible parked in the driveway. 'Tha-that's McBeth's ra-rented ka-car. He ma-made a ja-john ra-rent it for him and na-now he wa-won't re-re-re-return it.'

I watched as she scampered over to the car. It was red and impressive. She chirped the alarm off, then got in and lifted the tails of my shirt around her naked hips, and squatted on the driver's seat. She peed directly on the sheepskin upholstery.

When she was done, she got out and closed the door and chirped the alarm back on. Then she pranced back to the porch and shoved the keys through the mail slot in the door. Getting in the car beside me, she grabbed the Mad Dog bottle from between my legs and took a major slam. 'Let's ba-boogie,' she said.

The Starburst Motel is on La Brea Avenue near Sunset Boulevard. The marquee on top of the entrance in front advertises HBO-TV and kitchenettes, and there's a man-made sign taped to the outside of the Manager's Office window, 'DAILY SPECIAL $29.95.' Amy wanted a room with a kitchen, so I pulled in front and stopped by the office. Since my shakes were gone, I knew I was okay to go inside to the guy by myself.

As it turned out, if we wanted a room with a kitchen and HBO, it was thirty-nine dollars a day, ten dollars more for the kitchen. He had two rooms like that, and pets were no problem. One had a window and one was around back. Both rooms had air conditioning and were available. I looked at both and told Amy what I'd seen. It was an important deal to her and she guaranteed me that I could fist-fuck her if we'd take the nice room, the one with the window. What decided it for me was that the room was near the ice machine, which I considered an important feature.

It was two bucks more for a reason the guy mumbled in Urdu or Farsi. I took it for forty-one and paid an additional ten dollars for a key deposit, and then some more for tax and an additional eight dollars pet deposit fee. Sixty-three bucks total, when he got done adding.

I took care of it up front by putting seven days in advance on the credit card which had cleared telephone approval. I did it because I was concerned that, any minute, the card would be cancelled and a new one reissued in my wife's name only.

Later in the early afternoon, when we were moved in with all the food and stuff from the station wagon and the air conditioner was pumping away the Santa Ana heat, and we were part-way down the jug of Mad Dog and my brain was still working good, I discovered that Amy didn't stutter when she was drunk. As she put away more Mad Dog, her speech was less affected. Booze disconnected her stutterer.

She loved being able to talk, which, I now understood, was why she loved drinking. Without the stutter, there were books and buildings full of words that she wanted to say. They were sprayed in bunches around the motel room, like machine-gun fire in a James Bond movie.

I had to be told everything: her I.Q. was in the upper one-thirties. She was from Muncie, Indiana. She had received the fourth-best rating on the intelligence tests at her high school. (Celeste Depue edged her out for third by one point, but Celeste's mother was a dyke gym teacher at a girls' high school and Celeste was a twat that nobody liked, so not winning third prize wasn't a big deal.)

More and more words gushed forth, like subway passengers pouring into the trains at rush hour. It had been twelve weeks since she'd quit tenth grade and driven with her boyfriend, a greedy crack dealer, to Hollywood from Muncie. His nickname was 'Limp' because his right leg was two inches shorter than his left, a result of a motorcycle wreck when he was fourteen. After Limp dumped her, sticking her with two days' back rent in a rooming house on Selma Avenue and never returning, she and an older girlfriend started giving blow jobs to men in cars on Sunset Boulevard, where she met McBeth who let her stay in a spare room on a mattress at his house for fifty dollars a day. Limp had a cousin named Debbie whom Amy had met once at IHOP on Sunset.

Every night, Amy tried to get by the restaurant to see if she could find Debbie and persuade her to get a message to Limp: she was sorry that he'd seen her talking to Boyd down the hall that one and only time, because it really had meant nothing, but it probably was the reason Limp left that night without telling her or ever saying goodbye.

We drank more and I listened. The syllables came like desperate boat people begging for attention. She seemed to be trying to use every word she knew before she passed out, or got too drunk to talk.

I learned about her barmaid mother and her older sister, who were both drunks. About her abortion. About all the sadness and brutality and stupidity that happens to people when they're on the street and making it the best way they can – stories that I'd heard a hundred times in recovery programs or in hospital nuthouse lock-down wards. She talked and ate cookies, and we drank, while Rocco slept motionless at the end of the bed and I watched HBO with the sound off.

Amy'd read everything to make up for being homely and unable to communicate: History. Poetry. Fiction. Non-fiction. Crap. From Richard Nixon's memoirs to Donald Trump to Og Mandino and Irving Wallace. Two or three books a week since she was ten years old. Her passions were penises and books.

She knew my guys too: Hubert Selby, Hemingway, Steinbeck, e.e. cummings, Eugene O'Neill. Her favorite writer was William Faulkner. When she was drinking, she talked like he wrote.

After most of the first bottle was gone, she became grateful and wanted to oblige my sexual needs, even though I didn't really have any. She was highly-skilled as a cocksucker and began performing energetically on me for a couple of minutes, and then stopped because she realized that the sucking interfered with what she wanted to say about how good she was at giving head, so the blow job turned into a hand job to enable her to continue speaking.

After a while, I talked about my wife's credit card that was about to be cancelled, and she interrupted to explain to me how Limp would 'work' his customers to help them get cash advances on their plastic beyond their credit card limit. She'd assisted him, and made several of the calls herself. She offered to do the same for me.

Amy used the room phone to make the call, saying that she was Mrs. Bruno Dante and explaining to a local bank manager which honored the card about how much short-term cash we needed, because we wanted to buy a rare Queen Anne table for our living room but we didn't have the money until we could get back to New York and transfer funds. I thought she was overdoing it when she told the guy about our bad luck with food poisoning on our first trip to Los Angeles, and about how we preferred Universal Studios to Disneyland, because it had more live attractions for the kids.

He put her on hold and checked the payment history on the card, or whatever they do, then came back on the line and said okay. I got dressed and we drove down to the bank to pick up the twenty-five hundred in cash before it closed at 4:00 p.m.

Because we got the money, I kept on with the wine three more days and stayed in the room trying to stop my brain. I was beginning to realize that my father was dead. I kept the blinds closed and the TV tuned in to HBO and the other movie stations.

On the first afternoon, I tried to write a poem for the old man. It had been years. What came out was awful. No good. It had been too long. I stopped because the wine was a higher priority.

Amy was too young to drive, but by checking the phone book, we found a liquor store around on Sunset that would deliver food and booze right away if we tipped good. She took charge of that, and walking Rocco too.

Being in the room drinking Dog was all that I wanted to do. But on the second day, I began having time lapses again. Chunks of hours got lost, and I knew that the wine was turning on me again. But I was in too deep to back out. It got worse, and sleep became almost impossible, so I drank more wine.

If I did drift off, I would wake up in a few minutes, after having the same dream with the marching death squad in my brain – the same beaks of huge black birds on their faces.

Twelve or twenty hours passed. I was awake, but not awake.

Amy filled me in the next day. I had talked about death, and we had watched a Claude Rains movie. Also, I had called my ex-shrink in New York to say I was choking on my own gloom for the last time, but there had been no actual conversation because an answering service lady had picked up my call. Then Amy told me that we had walked to the newsstand, where I became a lunatic because I thought the guy had tried to short-change me on a fifty-dollar bill. I'd pulled down a rack full of magazines off the shelf and thrown them into the street. It all happened, but I recalled zip.

Amy had become afraid and made me call Fabrizio later that night. Me and Fab had had a half-hour conversation in which I had made an admission and an apology for bashing his Country Squire, then a promise to return the car. She said Fab and I had discussed the funeral the next day and that I'd promised my brother I'd be there.

My memory was a complete blank, but when it was light outside the next morning, Amy woke up and repeated to me all of what my end of the conversation had been and the other events that occurred. After the call, she made me stop the wine so I was able to take a shower. Then I drank several cold beers to prevent a slam.

In a while, conscious, I started seeing a thousand evil snakes with human legs eating away the backs of my eyes and I felt a hot, jagged, twenty-two-caliber bullet hole drilled through my head from temple to temple. The hole was being flossed by a bicycle chain.

I puked for a long time, then took four aspirin and half a bottle of pink liquid for my gut. Amy force-fed me cold pizza and finally I slept okay for a few hours.

*   *   *

While I was getting dressed to go to the funeral, Amy wanted me to talk about my relationship with my father since she had no memory of her own dad. What did it feel like to have a father and then have him die? I said that the old man and I were never close – that we lived three thousand miles apart, but that the space between us was immeasurable. We were composed of different colors: me, green; him red or blue. We had not ever connected, and I'd been a big disappointment in his life. I said that I didn't feel anything, but Amy inspected my eyes and said that what she saw in them was pain.

I left the motel in the Ford station wagon and followed Sunset Boulevard as it twisted and turned the whole distance to the Pacific Coast Highway. Then I headed north to Malibu. It was a slower way to go, but I didn't feel solid enough to drive on the freeway. Amy stayed behind with Rocco and watched HBO movies.

Chapter Twelve

OUR LADY OF Malibu Church is a redwood A-frame deal built up against the hills at the ocean end of Malibu Canyon in the late nineteen forties. When I was a kid, the hard oak pews were always stinging cold from the wet sea air, and the grey tile floor was waxed to an icy gloss. A perfect spot for God. And all the topics that were talked about from the pulpit by Father Brundage had only one thing in common – they were unrelated to the experience of regular human beings. As I drove by, looking for a place to park, I saw members of my family standing on the steps, in front, near the limos and the hearse. Not wanting anyone to see me, or the dents I'd put in my brother's wagon, I located a spot on the street down the block behind an RV.

I sat with the windows up and smoked until past the time for everyone to be inside. My mind had been critically missing the wine it needed to stay quiet, and now filled itself with thoughts of madness and imminent disaster. Panic glued me to the seat of the car.

When I was finally able to go in, I stood by the holy water at the foyer entrance and let the iciness of the place mix with my sweat-soaked clothes. I breathed in and out and steadied myself.

The mass had started, but the temple's pews were mostly empty, except for the backs of the heads of a solid line of the Dante family and my wife Agnes. They occupied half a row up front near the coffin. My stomach wrenched at the sight of seeing my wife.

There was a scattering of a dozen or so others in the church – I recognized some Malibu neighbors, a famous L.A. writer who admired my father's out-of-print books, a sitcom director, and a few of my father's screenwriter associates. I didn't have to look to know that the expression on the cold meat in the open coffin would not be Dante's, but some peculiar rendering of him that Mom and Fab and a bent ecclesiastical mortician had invented to mollify reality.

My hand was shaking and resisted dipping itself into the clammy wetness of the holy water urn, but an instinct of compliance made me do it anyway. As I did, someone behind me put his fingers in too.

Turning, I recognized my father's old neighbor, Townsend O'Hagen, wearing an out-of-date pin-striped business suit and a red-band fedora in honor of the occasion. Seeing him helped calm me down.

During the anti-communist McCarthy hearings in the fifties, Townsend was blacklisted as a screenwriter and then made it worse for himself by naming names in front of the committee on TV, to save his own ass. According to Dante it ruined his movie career forever.

I'd thought him dead, because no one in my family had mentioned his name for years, ever since he had moved out of Malibu and opened a used-book store in Santa Monica. He looked swell. Prosperous. He was at least eighty. He smiled at me and I smiled back.

He even managed to remember my name from when I'd gone to grammar school with his daughter, Kerry. 'You're Bruno,' he whispered. 'Know who I am?' I smiled and nodded and said, 'Sure, Townie O'Hagen.'

He extended his condolences about my father, then followed

behind me down the center aisle, where I sat next to my sister and Benny Roth in the family row. Townie occupied the next pew back, across from Paul Matsumoto, my father's movie agent.

The whole thing was over in half an hour, with everyone's thoughts and Brundage's prayers bouncing off the varnished casket. When the sad family, all dressed in black, had filed out down the aisle and stood outside in front of the church, the other attendees came up and gave Mom and my sister hugs. Fabrizio stood up tall in his Armani suit ($900 at May Company) and shook people's hands.

I stayed to the side, cowering, smoking cigarettes and talking to Townsend and my cousin John, a helluva film cameraman as well as a crackerjack auto mechanic. John gave me some mechanical pointers about what to look for in buying a used American car. Talking with them helped a little to quiet the jeering, critical voices in my mind.

Standing there, too near my own feelings, close to panic, I impulsively hugged my mother and lied, saying I had an appointment about a job and was not going with them. Then I kissed my sister, Maggie, and shook Fab's hand and apologized again. He took his car keys back but wouldn't meet my eyes or talk to me.

I was about to walk away, not considering my mode of transportation back to L.A., when Townsend mentioned that he was living in a rented duplex up in Benedict Canyon, 'near the precise location shown on the Maps Of The Stars' Homes where Valentino publicly inseminated his first horse.' He asked if I wanted a ride.

As we were leaving, my wife confronted me, insisting that I explain my absence from her over the last four days. While my mother and my family looked on, she loudly hissed her demand for a divorce and accused me of being a drug addict and an AIDS carrier, stealing her credit card and ruining her life.

It was cause enough for me to lose control, scream, and act crazy on the front steps of the church. My brother-in-law, Benny Roth, stepped in to calm me down, and Agnes backed off, realizing that she'd picked the wrong time, politically, to start any shit.

In a few minutes, she and my family were packed aboard the limos, ready to go to the graveyard. I located Townsend across the parking lot, waving me toward him from behind the wheel of his old Caddy convertible. I got in and we headed back toward Hollywood.

Being away from the coffin and the church made me feel better. Near Topanga Canyon, I asked Townie to stop for cigarettes at a liquor store. I came out with the smokes and a jug of Shenley's for the two of us. At first, he turned me down, but after a couple of nips on the bottle, he was in a good mood and started singing, 'Tura Lura Lura' and the Latin version of, 'Oh Come All Ye Faithful.' He did them both in a heavy Dublin accent, as we passed the whiskey bottle across the seat to each other.

The whiskey made him chatty, and he had lots of stories he wanted to tell me about the famous actresses and production secretaries he and Robin Hood had partied with.

Townie was a wonderful storyteller and his voice reverberated like an announcer on an old-time radio drama. Fights, week-long drunks, ex-wives with knives, lawsuits, jails. He filled the car with poetry. Most of what he said was exaggerated, but it was magic.

Then he got serious, and said it was important for me to know how it was for movie writers like him and Jonathan Dante fifty years ago in L.A. So he filled me in about how the contract system at the studios worked, and how the producers were permitted to mistreat the in-house screenwriters before there was a union. Writers had no say whatever.

When I asked about the blacklist, he didn't want to talk about it at first. Then, he took a big snort, changed his mind, and started in. He had gone to two or three 'sympathetic' meetings because he'd been invited to attend by an actress with big tits whom he'd been trying to date. According to Townsend, these gatherings were 80% cocktail party and 20% talk. Harmless stuff, a threat to no one. But names were taken down, and later that list got people into trouble.

He said that Dante was lucky, because he had always refused to join groups and did not want to be identified with the Hollywood egos, insincerity and bullshit. The old man never got involved.

After World War II the film business hit a slump. Influence, and whom you knew at the studio, were important in getting the good writing assignments. My father was what Townsend called, 'reverse-blacklisted.' It happened because he refused to be part of any 'in' groups or hang out socially with the 'right' people. Townsend laughed and said that my father's 'good luck' was that he'd been too blunt with people, had changed agents a lot, and had a reputation for a bad temper. Kissing ass was impossible for Dante. Once, he'd even punched out the producer, Val Lewton.

Townsend remembered that my father had spent the next couple of years, until 1951, writing a novel, without a screen assignment. But eventually, a desperate producer with a handful of money and a tight shooting schedule called, needing a 'safe' screenwriter to rework a botched script.

When we crossed Sunset, heading north on La Brea, I showed Townsend where to drop me off by the Starburst Motel. I handed him the jug, and when he took a last, long pull and brought it down, I saw tears in his eyes. He and my father were from the other city. The L.A. that was gone forever. 'You remind me of him,' he said. 'You have his disposition . . . May the road rise up to meet you.'

I said, 'Thanks for the ride.'

By the time the car door swung open, he was smiling again and shook my hand. When he pulled out, his driver's window was down, and I heard him start to sing the first notes of a Christmas tune from a mindless forties movie whose name I couldn't remember.

Rocco was sick. He snarled when we tried to pet him or come near his food dish. Amy said that he hadn't eaten much of anything since his fight, and that most of the time he was just sleeping. I went out again and walked to the liquor store, where I bought a carton of milk and some Mogen David wine and a quart size of Jack Daniels. I remembered that dogs like milk.

On the shelf with the magazines was a whole section of newspapers and fold-up publications that advertised used cars for sale. I purchased the thickest one, containing the most ads.

When we tried to get Rocco to drink some of the milk in his bowl, he refused. Then Amy heated a panful on the stove, put whiskey in it, and he drank over half the contents before going back to sleep. Her mother had owned dogs, and Amy said that she could tell from experience when something was wrong. 'Ha-he's in pa-pain,' she said. 'Th-th-that's wh-wh-why he da-dada-da-drank th-tha-that sha-shit. Da-dog's da-da-don't na-normally da-drink wa-wine or wha-wha-wha-wha-whiskey. Ha-he's sa-sick.'

When I opened a new bottle of Mad Dog, she told me that she would leave if I wouldn't promise to stay off wine. I agreed that I would, which I knew was a good thing anyway. I tried to read an old novel by Daniel Mainwaring but my mind kept drifting to thoughts of my father. It had been a long time since I'd thought seriously about writing a poem, but I wanted to try. Half an hour later, pages from a yellow legal pad littered the motel room floor. The stuff was pretentious and self-conscious. Not poetry. Worse than Ferlinghetti's worst, most contrived, pompous, insane, drug-crazed nonsense drool. It confirmed to me that I was a liar and an imposter, certainly not a poet.

Amy was sure that I was too critical and wanted me to read one of them to her and bribed me with the promise of a blow job. I attempted a delivery of the best one out loud but it was so bad that I stopped in the middle in disgust and threw the torn shreds of it across the room. She laughed at me, but she sucked my dick anyway, with long, tingling, deep up and down gulps until I blasted off to Mars.

It wasn't a Japanese car. It was a six-cylinder American Dodge Dart. A 1971 model with the 225-cubic-inch motor. Someone once told me – a New York cabbie, I think – that the slant six Chrysler-made engine was the best, most reliable car motor ever made.

This one was supposed to have fifty-five thousand miles on it. Rebuilt. Carlos from El Salvador had a backyard jammed with eight or ten old clunkers, with their hoods up in varying stages of repair. They looked like hungry, rusted dinosaurs. We weaved our way through half a dozen cars until he led us to the Dodge. He smiled and pointed it out like an old friend, 'Is best one,' he said. 'This one run like Mercedes Benz.'

He was tall for a Latin, at least six feet, and he had a high regard for his sales ability. He told us that he made his living by fixing up old cars. He owned a solid gold front tooth and smiled too much.

In El Salvador, Carlos said that he had been the equivalent of a head mechanic at a new car agency. Amy seemed impressed. He said that if I bought the car, he would repair whatever went wrong with the motor for the next six months, at no charge. Then he smiled to verify his sincerity. Amy smiled back representing our side.

The Dart had an automatic transmission and the body was second or third generation dark blue. The tires were all good, and all four hubcaps were still on the wheels. Both doors had minor dings and part of the grille was missing, but on the whole, it looked decent.

Inside, on the seats, there were worn and unhappy beige imitation sheepskin covers that concealed the twenty-eight-year-old ruined plastic covers that had come with the car. That was okay. All the buttons and knobs were on the dash and the AM-FM radio played a favorite old Jimmy Reid blues tune when I clicked it on. I believed the song to be a good omen.

The taxi ride we took to Downey from Hollywood to buy the car had cost thirty-eight dollars, plus tip. I gave Carlos and his gold tooth $1,200 in cash after a good test drive that put the Dart through her paces. The twenties and tens I peeled off made his tooth grin. The expenditure left me just under four hundred dollars in total assets.

Amy had been sipping Jack Daniels on the ride there, because she knew that she would be talking to strangers and wanted to control her stutter. But she'd overdone it. The side effect was that the bitch became too friendly, and an irritating flirtation between her and the oily-haired mechanic developed. I attempted to ignore the slutty nonsense until Carlos's attention started to wander. While he tallied up my cash, she caused him to lose count and leer at the crotch of her tight elastic black pants. The transaction got sidetracked.

'Pardon me,' I said to break it up.

'What, honey?' Amy whispered back in a silky voice contrived to impress the blue-eyed mechanic. She wasn't stutter-
ing.

My mouth was angry. 'Have you decided to blow this
wetback before I buy the car or will you be gracious enough
to wait until he's finished taking my money?'

It was poor word selection. She was instantly angry. 'Fa-fuck
you, Bruno. You're such a nasty pig. I da-don't owe you
anything!'

In too deep, I had to go on. 'If she sucks your dick, Carlos, I
want fifty bucks taken off the price of the car. Fair enough?'

Carlos had stopped smiling.

On the drive back to Hollywood in the Dart, she took on
the part of the violated heroine, sitting in the rear seat with
Rocco's face in her lap. Amy gulped whiskey and spit words
at the back of my head like a riled cobra.

'You're a mean-ass know-it-all pa-prick, Bruno. A bad-
tempered wa-wino fa-fuck . . . so much smm-mm-smarter than
everybody else. I'd rather have herpes and fuck Ka-Ka-Carlos
and push a supermarket ka-ka-cart ka-ka-collecting a-lu-lu-
luluminum beer ka-cans and sa-sleeping in da-doorways on
Hollywood Boulevard than ta-ta-take another day of your shit.
I don't la-love you anymore, and additionally, I ha-hate your
ga-guts.' When Amy was angry, even if she was drunk, her
speech impediment became more pronounced.

Her anger had lost most of its steam in a few minutes, and
she satisfied herself by muttering to the dog. After that, she was
silent, brooding and smoking the rest of the way to Hollywood.

When I had gotten off the freeway and stopped for a traffic
light a mile from the motel, without warning, she lurched the
back door open and got out of the car. The Jack Daniels bottle
lay empty next to the dog.

'Hey, get in,' I yelled.

'Fuck you, nasty prince dickface!' she shouted back, wobbling. 'Fuck your whole da-dead unsociable fa-family! You owe me $800. Two hundred a day for four days. Pay me!'

We were two lanes from the curb. 'Goddammit, Amy, get in the car!'

'No way,' she screamed, pounding hard with her open hand on the metal roof. 'You fucked me fa-four days! One!' POUND. 'Two!' POUND. 'Three!' POUND. 'Four!' POUND. 'That's eight hundred dollars!' POUND – POUND – POUND. The echoing noise started Rocco barking and snarling.

I yelled back, trying to reason with her, 'You'll get us arrested if you keep that up! You know I haven't got eight hundred dollars!'

'Not my problem!' POUND – POUND. 'Your problem! Ya-your own father loved you but because it w-wasn't your wa-way, you sta-stiffed him too.' POUND-POUND. 'Ba-bad tempered asshole! Ice dick!'

Her hammering finally made me angry. I got out of the driver's side to stop her. Cars were speeding dangerously close.

Seeing me coming, drunk and unafraid, she pushed the rear door closed and weaved her way by an oncoming pick-up to get to the sidewalk, laughing and screaming at the same time. She enjoyed taunting me. 'You can't even ta-take care of a fa-fucking dog!'

I decided to let her go. She was too drunk and too crazy and angry. I got back in the car and watched her stumble north in the direction of Sunset Boulevard, yelling curses at me over her shoulder.

Chapter Thirteen

ROCCO'S HEALTH WAS worse. All that day, he lay in the same spot on the motel room floor without moving. If he tried to get up, he'd yelp in pain. The next morning, he refused to eat anything I offered him, or even to drink any milk and whiskey. Amy had not returned, and my relationship with the dog had now become one of icy tolerance.

The Dart's tank needed gas and I needed cigarettes. I left the dog in the room with the TV on and an open box of Oreo cookies.

At the self-service gas station, I counted all the money in my pants. Paying the rent for another full week would leave me just over a hundred dollars. I remembered that Amy's clothes were still in the closet on the floor in a plastic bag. The manager would hold them for her if I checked out. But finding a place that took dogs and had a lower daily rent would be hard to do. Either way, I'd be broke in a few days. I made a decision to go to the movies, eat popcorn and not think about it.

That night on the way back to the motel, I stopped at the liquor store to pick up a jug and a copy of the *L.A. Times*. I wanted to see what was available in the Employment Section. Once I had the paper, I went by the store's cold cuts department and selected a twelve-ounce package of expensive bologna for Rocco. I felt bad about leaving him alone in the unlit room for so many hours.

When I got back to the motel, I opened the cold cuts, shredded several pieces, then dumped them into his bowl. He ignored the offering at first, so I added milk and pushed the dish against his nose. He still was unmoved.

Then I poured in a little whiskey, less than an ounce. He evaluated my submission with a snort and a tentative swipe of his big pink tongue – a master chef sampling the broth of his underling apprentice. It pleased him enough that he ate about half the contents of the bowl, while looking up at me from time to time as if to make sure that I understood he was doing me a favor.

I was almost out of money and I needed an income. A job. Opening the *L.A. Times*, I had the idea of bartender positions first, thinking that I might be lucky enough to earn money pouring drinks. I'd done it before at two different saloons in New York, until it had become clear that fighting was an important component of the trade.

There were only six small ads in the bartender section, anyway. Five were for more formal restaurant and hotel work, upscale stuff. The last was in another area code. Away from Hollywood. A bartender needs to be no further than walking distance from work. I gave up the idea.

Next I looked at advertisements for boiler rooms. 'Telemarketing.' I hoped that I could make myself do it again. The money was always fast, and hammering customers with preposterous come-on lies seemed to fit much better here in Los Angeles. With a couple of drinks in me, I could go back to guaranteeing color TVs and Hawaiian vacations, duping clerks and receptionists and assistant managers into receiving truck loads of photocopy toner cartridges, office supply seconds, gas station driveway cleaner, surplus cable and wire, tools, computer ribbon and guaranteed loans . . . 'Mrs. Washington, Bill Baxter with United Credit Consultants getting back to you . . . Your loan application is in the final approval stage right now. I'm almost sure we'll have the good news this week. We'll need you to send in your processing fee TODAY so we can complete our paperwork . . . I'll hold on while you get your check book . . . Of course it's guaranteed. We personally stand behind each and every loan . . .'

My problem was that I didn't know any phone room people here, and trying the wrong hustle could take a day or more potential income out of my pocket. There were no ads that promised the telemarketer a weekly guarantee or cash every day, so I decided it was safest to pass.

I worked a fresh pint halfway down looking through the other sections of the classified, circling possibilities, hating and fearing having to confront the ads.

From the 'Chauffeur,' 'Driver' and 'Clerk' columns I went to 'Trainees.' Nothing inspired me. Finally, back under 'Sales,' I came to a narrow, thin ad that looked fetching. Dream Mates International needed Counselor / Salespersons for their new office in Westchester. 'GUARANTEED DRAW PAID WEEKLY – HIGH COMMISSIONS – DAILY CASH BONUSES . . . Must have own car and be prepared to earn BIG $$$$!!! No previous experience necessary – WE TRAIN – Only serious and highly motivated need apply.'

There was a twenty-four-hour hotline number to call. I read through the ad twice more to be sure that I was highly motivated, then dialed the hotline.

A recording with instructions answered. A phone mail lady. She told me to punch a series of keys. I pressed those, then got more instructions, hit some more buttons, then heard a man's voice explain a long deal about how splendid being a counselor at DMI could be. The recording had high praise for a new guy named Glen Manoff. In his first full week, Glen had earned $1,000 in commission and bonuses. The message said that Mitch Glickman, the old-timer, made $3,000.

It was a long, sophisticated presentation dealing with the importance of video dating and the career path to financial independence at DMI.

I did what the voice requested and left my name, a call-back number and the message, 'I am a highly motivated career sales-man with a burning desire to achieve financial independence. Your DMI deal sounds like a path to success, fulfillment and greatness. I hope that you will call me back right away so that I can get on DMI's winning team.' I pressed the # key, the way the directions indicated and after a new voice wished me happy holidays, I hung up.

After the call, my head was pounding and my body was jerked full of adrenaline. Fear of employment. I didn't think anyone would call back from DMI, but I turned on the lights and went to the closet anyway. I would need the right clothes.

My sports jacket, the heavy grey tweed that I'd worn on the plane and to the funeral, looked passable. My only dark pants had a small noticeable rip at the bottom of the crotch. They were wrinkled and without a crease, but they'd be okay after a trip to the cleaners. I'd spilled something on my only dress shirt and tie and that stain appeared to be permanent and fatal, smelling like brake fluid. My daily brown shoes would look okay if they were polished.

The rest of that night I smoked, watched HBO and read poetry, not sleeping. The idea of a job again, after the treatment center and six months of unemployment, had my mind racing.

As I lay awake, I began to blame Rocco. Watching him curled up on the floor next to the warmth of a heating duct yelping in his sleep, I became aware that having him in my life was like strapping a wet sandbag to my ass. I was a prisoner to debt because of this animal.

By myself, I could sleep in the car and save three hundred a week in rent, but with my father's sick mutt as a dependent, I was now obliged to provide food and warmth as one would provide for a child.

What if the fucker with his evil breath had hip dysplasia, or needed tooth extractions, or had contracted doggie cancer requiring hundreds or thousands of dollars in veterinary expenses? What then? My brain spent the rest of the night exploring ways to be rid of the beast.

At 9:00 a.m., I got the animal shelter's number from the information operator. I dialed, a computer answered with instructions. I pressed, and entered my way into another phone system with hold intervals. A minute or so later, a live attendant finally came on the line. I hadn't slept in thirty hours.

'I know of a sick dog,' I said to the voice at the other end. 'He needs help. Veterinary attention.'

'We're not the vet, sir,' the guy said. 'We deal with homeless pets.'

'Then who do I call?'

'If you have a sick animal, call a vet.'

'I can't afford a vet. What if this dog were homeless? Would you take him then?'

'We'd come out and pick him up.'

'He's homeless. I'm moving. How does it work? How do we proceed?'

'We dispatch one of our personnel to come and get the dog . . . I'll need the animal's approximate weight, color and a general location of where he was last seen. What's the nearest major intersection to the location of the animal?'

'That's it?'

'Yes.'

'I'll give you the address . . . It's the Starburst Motel on La Brea Avenue just north of Sunset . . . What happens next? To the dog.'

'We'll pick him up and hold him for seventy-two hours or until somebody shows up to claim him. You are not the owner of the animal, correct?'

'Correct. What if nobody comes to get him?'

'After the mandatory seventy-two-hour period, we put the animal to sleep.'

'We can't do that.'

'. . . Sir, we're busy here. Are you reporting a stray dog?'

'He whimpers in his sleep all night and seems to be in a lot of pain. What's your recommendation?'

'Find his owner or bring him to the shelter.'

'His owner's dead. I'm in charge of the dog now.'

'How old is the animal?'

'Very old, maybe twelve or thirteen.'

'Have him put to sleep.'

'I can't do that. The dog belonged to my father.'

'Then take the animal to a vet.'

'I told you, I don't have the money for a vet.'

'I can't help you, sir.'

'I asked for a recommendation.'

'I just gave you one.'

'Go fuck yourself.'

After noon that day, my room phone rang and woke me up. At first I thought it was Amy, but it was Susan Bolke, Mr. Berkhardt's assistant from Dream Mates International. Susan was returning my message for the VP of sales. She sounded young and sexy and businesslike.

She said that Mr. Berkhardt had been impressed by my

message and had asked her to set an appointment with me for a job interview the next day. Susan gave me the address of the DMI office in Westchester. I puked for ten minutes, then took a long hot shower. It helped to quiet my mind.

Rocco wouldn't eat anything, but when I went to the door to leave, he got up and acted like he wanted to go too. I remembered what it was like to be locked alone in a room and decided to let him come with me. Me and this dog had things in common . . .

First, we walked in the direction of the cleaners down the block on Sunset. He was still limping, but stopped to pee ten or fifteen times. We even pissed together on the same shrub.

The window sign at the cleaners advertised, SAME DAY SERVICE in big letters as if SAME DAY SERVICE were the name of the shop. I decided to try my luck.

To clean and repair the trousers, the guy wanted $16.00. I negotiated in American, but he responded in a form of Asian, nodding his head up and down. When I asked how much it was for the tailoring alone, he nodded quickly many times and said $12.00. We arrived at an agreement to just do the cleaning, without the repair, but the price would be $6.00, 50% more because I wanted same day service. I nodded, and he nodded, and we closed the deal.

I helped Rocco climb into the back seat of the Dart and drove to the Pick & Save department store on Western Avenue. Inside, in the men's section, I found two manufacturer's-reject white dress shirts in a plastic package for $14.99, (you had to buy two.) They were made from a plastic miracle fabric that excluded cotton. I threw the shirts into my wire shopping basket and continued on.

Pick & Save specialized in odd merchandise. Close-outs, seconds, discontinued items. There were no neck ties in the men's section, but in the boys' aisle I found a display that had a number of different kinds. Most were too short, or unsuitable, because of the childish themes painted on their fronts. But I did find a dark blue clip-on with little galloping white pigs running hither and yon across the front. The tie went in the wire basket also.

In another department, I discovered a strange flow-on shoe polish for eighty-nine cents that must have failed badly as a marketing gimmick, because there were hundreds of the little sponge-topped bottles on a shelf twenty feet long. I selected a bottle of the 'Calico Brown,' and an additional one of the 'Ebony,' in case I ever expanded my wardrobe to include black shoes.

Chapter Fourteen

SUSAN BOLKE'S PERFUME was as sexy as her voice. She had a clipboard and protruding nipples and a frizzy hair style like the girl in the vaginal spray ad on TV. Everyone who worked at DMI dressed as if they were applying for a job. The men had double-breasted suits, and the women all wore panty hose and lots of jewelry.

Susan and I sat down on matching white leather love seats in the Dream Mates International lobby, and she explained the commission plan and the $250 per week guarantee that the company provided for the first two weeks.

She smiled approvingly when I put out my cigarette, and told me about the three-day training to fully learn the DMI presentation. Everything was based on my interview with Mr. Berkhardt. Berkhardt made the hiring decisions. She gave me compatibility statistics on the science of video dating and used the word demographics five or six times. I liked the $250 guarantee.

We chatted for a few more minutes, with Susan making occasional notes and checking off little boxes on her clipboard form. I noticed that my hands were shaking too much, and that I had yellow stains on my fingers from nicotine. She could see that I was self-conscious about the hands, but she kept smiling to put me at ease. Finally, I was given my own clipboard with a job application and a cheap pen. Then Susan left.

As I filled out the form, I watched a big TV mounted into the wall above the reception desk. It was playing dating interview videos of available single adults talking about their careers and their likes and dislikes. The volume was up too high. The people in the videos were normal and sincere-sounding. DMI was in pursuit of the affluent, upper-middle-income customer.

On most of the questions, I lied, or got impatient, or skipped the question all together. Filling it out was hard, because of my rattling fingers.

By the end of the form, my mind had convinced itself that I was a chump for driving all the way from Hollywood to compete in a wardrobe contest. I was out of my league and my form looked like it had been completed by a six-year-old. My father's dog was imprisoned in the car in the parking lot with the windows up, and I was having a vision of him eating the seat covers in a display of meanness for being left alone too long.

I decided to leave and call some of the telemarketing ads in the *L.A. Times*. Before I could return the clipboard to Susan, Morgan Berkhardt had come out of his office and was on his way toward me.

He looked like the boss. His suit was double-breasted and he had a big football player neck, and white teeth and a red-stone college graduation ring. He introduced himself and we shook hands. He took my completed job application and began going over my answers.

While he studied the questionnaire, I was distracted by a new client movie starting on the lobby TV. This one was different, not a dating video. It was of a marriage. I was close enough to the set to hear the announcer's voice-over. 'Every day, three hundred and sixty-five days a year, another Dream Mates International client is making a lifelong commitment of love. You could be too. Join DMI today.'

Morgan Berkhardt finished reading my application and saw me watching the video. 'Impressive marketing concept, isn't it, Mr. Dante?'

'Right! Imaginative too,' I heard my ass-kissing mouth reply.

'Please come with me.' I followed him across a floral carpet, to a fancy oak door with a brass handle that led into his office. We went in and sat down. He, on the other side of a big oak desk, and I, in a small, thin-legged armchair.

On the shelves behind Berkhardt's leather chair were books and packaged motivational tape programs. I'd read sales and self-help stuff at my first visit to St. Joseph of Cupertino's recovery ward, because there'd been nothing else to do after ten o'clock when they shut off the TV. For weeks, I'd been unable to sleep, so I'd stay up reading all night. Tommy Hopkins. Og Mandino. Charles Roth.

I could see that Berkhardt was a big Brian Tracy fan. Several of Brian's tape programs were in Berkhardt's collection on the shelf. Tracy stresses boldness as a success key, so I decided to be assumptive in my interview with Morgan Berkhardt.

'Bruno,' he said looking up from my application, 'Can I call you Bruno?'

'Sure. Can I call you Morgan?'

'If you'd like.'

'I see you're a Brian Tracy fan, Morgan?'

'Yes, I am.'

'I thought *The Psychology of Success* was an important work. I like his systematic approach to personal growth.'

'I'm impressed, Bruno. Very few of the people that interview in this office know Brian Tracy's material.'

'I'm not surprised, Morgan. It's been my observation that the majority, the run of the mill, the average, the sheep on the street and the piss-poor are too lazy to get off their fat uncommitted asses and do what it takes to be successful. Personal growth requires a commitment, we both know that. One must grasp life by the vitals and yank. Personally, I've made inspired decisions based on the information in some of those books. I want to be a winner.'

'Glad to hear it, Bruno.'

'Darn right. Absolutely.'

'By the way, you must have filled in some incorrect dates here in the employment history section. There are some inconsistencies in your information.'

'I apologize for that oversight, Morgan.'

'I'm a little confused. You were in telemarketing with the same company for twelve years, correct?'

'Correct, Morgan. Same job. They went tits-up so I relocated here to Los Angeles. New city, new opportunities. Fresh start. Taking the decisive approach.'

'A good work history is important. What did you sell at Omni Incorporated?'

'Computer products. Diskettes. Mag tape. Data processing supplies.'

'Twelve years at one position is a major commitment.'

'Thanks, Morgan. I pride myself on my loyalty, dependability and job execution. I feel I'm a go-getter. Is that what you're looking for at DIM?'

'DMI. You're a writer, too?'

'Yes, Morgan.' My fucking hands were beginning to shake uncontrollably, so I anchored one under my thigh and clamped the other one under an armpit.

'Interesting. What type of things do you write?'

'Poems, Morgan. But I gave it up when I decided to channel all my career energy into sales and marketing.'

'Books of poems?'

'No. Excessive, self-indulgent odds and ends, mostly.'

'Were any of your poems published?'

'Yes. In magazines and periodicals. But it's been a long time since I've had anything in print.'

'Not a lot of millionaire poets, are there?'

'That's why I'm here, Morgan.'

'Although you have a good telephone sales record, you really have no work background for the type of position DMI is offering.'

'I see it differently, Morgan. I'm here to lock on to a career where I can distinguish myself and become financially independent. My background shows I'm highly motivated and I bust my ass. I take no prisoners when I'm working on the phone, and I can slam a mooch with the best of 'em. Frankly speaking, I'm sure that I'm the type of person you're looking for to join the DMI team.'

'According to the dates on your application you were a writer for fifteen years. A poet.'

'Okay. Correct.'

'That shows a total of twenty-seven years of employment. Do you see why I'm confused.'

'I made a mistake, for chrissake. I get impatient sometimes when I'm completing complicated forms. I don't lie on job applications. Am I being execrated here? Are you implying that I falsify information?'

'No.'

'Good.'

'You seem nervous? Aggressiveness is a good quality, but I need to do my job, Bruno. I have several more questions.'

I was suddenly on my feet, unable to stop myself. 'I want to get to the point here, Morgan, because I'm anxious not to lose time in my job search en route to my success. Bottom line, I could sell this deal with my eyes shut and whistle "Yankee Doodle Dandy" out my asshole at the same time. I'm an A-1 candidate.'

'Please sit down!'

'Let's cut to the chase. Yes or no? When can I start?'

'Will you sit down and follow direction!'

'What about today?'

He got to his feet. 'Look, I'm losing my patience.'

I sat down. My shirt was wet with sweat and my stomach was in a knot. 'I'm trying to make an impression here,' I said. 'I want this job.'

Before I left Berkhardt's office, he told me that he would make a decision about who he was hiring later that day, and that Susan Bolke would call me back at the number listed on my job application if I had been accepted.

It was past dark when I got back to my room at the Starburst Motel. I had overmedicated my nerves with two pints of Jack on the way back, after stopping at a used-book store on Venice Boulevard.

I could tell that Amy had been in the room. Rocco knew it too. He sniffed and snorted and wouldn't sit down.

Opening the closet door, I looked on the floor for her plastic bag of clothes. It was gone.

In the bathroom, there was a note stuck to the mirror with a glob of lipstick. The words appeared to be lyrics from a song from somewhere.

Bruno . . .

> You can drag your laundry down First Avenue
>> Then spend some time in your drugstore mind
> It's not what you think, it's what you do
>> I've got a pair of socks I like better than you.
>>> Thanks, but no thanks,
>>>> Amy

The light on my phone was blinking, so I went up to the office to find out who had called.

The night manager handed me the pink message slip. It was from Susan Bolke. I read the words and let my mind re-smell her perfume and see her fat nipples against her sheer blouse.

I was to report at Dream Mates International the next morning at 8:00 a.m. for a two-day training. I had the job. I went back to my room and watched TV.

Chapter Fifteen

IT WAS WEDNESDAY morning, two weeks before Christmas. The conference table in the DMI Training Room was full. A dozen of us. Mostly men. We were told that it would take two twelve-hour days to learn to sell the program. I was guaranteed a paycheck for the next two Fridays, and the company would be paying for lunch and dinner, which would be brought in.

Berkhardt's job was to show us DMI's success formula. He seemed to think that I had potential, because I was quick to grasp the material and asked a lot of questions.

Rocco stayed in the Dart. I parked it in the shade of a tree and lowered the front windows down a few inches. I'd walk him during the breaks, with my styrofoam coffee cup filled with Ralph's plain-wrap Vodka. I'd slam gulps while he pissed on the shrubs. The first afternoon, as I was securing his leash, he surprised me with a kiss. A big, wet lick across my nose and cheek. He was starting to like me.

On our walk, we passed outside the corner of the building where Ms. Bolke's desk was located. She saw us through the glass wall and waved, a kind of 'hiya schmuck' acknowledgement she reserved for the male trainees and lowlifes that earned less than 50 grand a year. I waved back.

On the second day, Berkhardt brought Mitch Glickman into the conference room so he could show the trainees photocopies of Mitch's last few paychecks. Five and six and seven thousand for two weeks work. $175K per year. Mitch was the top guy at the Westchester office, with his own personal sales team of six men. He'd been with the company three years. He had a big grin and contempt for everyone.

That night, at the end of the course, at Berkhardt's instructions, Mitch invited some of the male trainees to a live nude bar on Century Boulevard to celebrate. I locked Rocco in the Dart and rode with Mitch in his black Porsche. During my probationary period, I'd be assigned to Mitch's sales team.

He paid for everything – admission *and* liquor. After a few drinks, the others had gone and Mitch was drunk. He confided to me how he had been offered the position as Franchise Manager – first, before Berkhardt – and had turned it down, and how Susan Bolke had given him a hand job in the supplies closet at the DMI Thanksgiving party. It was important to Mitch to let me know that he owned four condos and a shopping center, and that his girlfriend was once a centerfold.

While we talked, he was getting up every few minutes to horn cocaine in the men's room. He'd come back to sit down and sniff and wipe his nose, then say something cool to the dancer at our end of the bar, and proceed to tell me more about himself. On our way out, he tipped the girl bringing drinks a hundred-dollar bill. I noted to myself that Mitch was a chump and good for a couple hundred anytime I needed it.

DMI contacted all its sales leads during the day, over the telephone; and each counselor would have two sales demos per evening.

In the afternoon, all the counselors would attend a sales meeting at 4:30, then pick up their leads. Berkhardt gave an extended pep talk rap about haves and have-nots and had each counselor declare which category he belonged in. When he came to me, I put my hand up. I was in all the way.

That night, my first assignment was a cook at Denny's

Restaurant. He turned out to be a no-show. I called the DMI office from a phone stand at the restaurant, and Berkhardt instructed me to report early for the second lead.

That was Ms. Tara Kerns of Redondo Beach. She lived in a five-year-old condominium complex with a Burger King on the corner and a Nissan dealer across the street. I remembered the old Datsun slogan, 'WE ARE DRIVEN' and felt inspired.

After I parked the car, I hammered a few gulps of my Ralph's Vodka, then splashed on some cologne to cover the smell of the booze. Leaving Rocco a few broken Oreos in his bowl, I locked the car and got my DMI demo kit out of the trunk. It consisted of a portable VCR and a case of videos featuring prospective male clients. I left the player behind, because on the lead form the box, 'HAS OWN VCR' had been checked 'YES.'

Ms. Kerns' lead form said she fell into the $60/$75K a year income area, which easily put her into the 'A' category. She owned her own uniform shop and had been divorced for eleven years. According to another checked box on the lead form, Tara liked sports and had all three major credit cards. It was just sundown when I knocked on the door to condo number one-twenty-eight.

The woman that opened the door was 6'3" in her heels and weighed at least 225. She had bright red hair and red lipstick and feet as big as a man's. My head came to just below her chin as we stood facing each other.

Coming early was lucky. As it turned out, Tara was five fingers down a fifth of Walker's Black Label. She had a glass in her hand and, in the background, I could see the open bottle and a dish full of ice on the wet bar. The booze gave the big woman a kind of sweetness and ease that some people get with drinks. I knew the stage. From where she was, you usually get drunk and quiet, or drunk-and-don't-give-a-shit. After I told her who I was and said I was early, she invited me in.

We sat down, I on her couch and Tara across in a chair. I noticed that she had a five-gallon, old-fashioned glass water-jug half-filled with change. All silver. No pennies. She had been paying bills because her checkbook was on the table with several stamped envelopes. A good sign.

I put my demo kit on the floor by the coffee table. Through the glass top I could see a sexy lingerie catalog under the table. A *Wheel of Fortune* program was blasting on the TV. The noise was intrusive. A fat, asshole lady was winning and screaming.

'How about a drink?' Tara asked.

'Thanks. Yes, I don't mind,' I said back, knowing it was a violation of DMI conduct requirements to use alcohol with a client. 'By the way, do you think it'd be okay if we turned down the TV? I think your dating future will be more interesting.'

She clicked the sound down with the remote control and made an accommodating face. 'Better?' she asked.

I said, 'Thanks.'

While Tara went to the kitchen to get my drink, I opened my kit with the videos of the ten most affluent male clients. I'd watched them all in the training. In my mind, I had already picked two that featured big ex-jocks, knowing they would be perfect for Tara Kerns.

She came back and set my drink down. Scotch with ice, not too much ice.

Maintaining professionalism is a big deal with DMI, and I wanted to do a good job. Pulling the Compatibility Question-naire from my case, I attached it to a clipboard. While I was filling in her name and address on the form, Tara switched the TV channel to a sitcom and jacked up the sound.

'No mama's boys,' she said, half snatching the board with the paper. Then she clicked the sound down again.

'Okay,' I said.

'I've been burned and I know what I want. What about male clients that are wimps or pansies? How would a prospective female customer discover that from watching a video?'

I took a hit from my drink. 'I don't know,' I said.

'No mama's boys or pansies, okay?'

'We don't label them like that,' I said. Then I heard my mouth announce, 'Why not try a biker bar? You can find all the parolees and scumbags you want. My company specializes in compatible single adults.'

'You don't have to be rude. You guys charge up the behind. I just want to get my money's worth. What if I start dating someone and discover that we're incompatible? What then?'

'Marry 'em. That's what I did.'

She set her drink down and looked me in the eye for several seconds. 'How long have you been a dating service salesman,' she asked.

'You mean how long have I been a counselor for Dream Mates International?'

'Yes. Doing this. How long?'

'Twenty minutes.'

We both laughed.

I understood some things about Tara. I have sorted self-made women into two kinds: the first is the kind that feels she has to beat and defeat all comers, especially men, and prove how capable she is. It's always a survival match. Kind number two is the type that has achieved some success because of being a good person and busting her ass like everyone else, and getting lucky the way we do sometimes. Tara, I was sure, was the second kind. Big and self-conscious and affectionate, like a red-lipped Irish Setter. Her toughness was air.

Drinking loosened her up, so I decided to deal with her in an up-front, straightforward way and get right down to business. But our questionnaire bored her, and I could tell that she'd had too much whiskey. She now appeared to be leering at me and checking me out.

As a kid, I remember peeling the paper off a stick of Juicy Fruit gum and not chewing it, but running the surface against the wetness of my tongue until all the sugar was dissipated, then turning it over and doing the same thing on the other side. Knowing the sweetness was there, but delaying the pleasure as long as possible. I was a stick of gum to Tara Kerns.

I needed the job. I had a guaranteed check coming on Friday. I had a sick dog to feed, and keeping a place to sleep other than my Dart was a good idea. Tara's checkbook was still open on the table. I was afraid if I fucked her I would lose the sale. I tried to pull the presentation together.

We finished the questionnaire, but I could tell by her answers that my client control had turned to shit. Her interest level wasn't high at all now, and I'd allowed the deal to get off track with so many drinks. 'Let's watch a video,' I said.

'In a minute,' she said, getting up, smiling, showing her big white teeth with lipstick stains, slurring her words. 'I'll top up our glasses first.'

I had a movie of Philip Kessler plugged in on the TV when she came back. On the label of the video box, they tell you the client's name and a few outstanding characteristics. Phil was 6'7" and weighed three hundred pounds. A dentist and a divorcee.

Tara handed me a half-full glass of whiskey and ice and sat down next to me on the couch, instead of on her chair.

'You're sloshed,' I said.

'Yes, I am.'

'I'm trying to do my job. This is my first presentation. Either we do business, or I leave.'

'Okay. I do business all day. Business is fine.'

'I want you to see someone who's your physical type, okay?'

'Okay,' she said, still leering.

The video started with Philip describing himself. I'd forgotten that Phil was arrogant and bald. 'My name is Philip Kessler. Doctor Philip Kessler. I'm thirty-eight years old and I like movies and dancing and I was an avid tennis player until my knee injury . . . ha, ha . . . I own my own boat docked in Marina del Rey, and I spend my spare time sailing . . . I have a condo and a ski-lodge at Mammoth . . .'

I stopped the video with the remote. Tara looked disgusted. 'What do you think?' I asked.

Her slurring was heavier. 'Mama's boy . . . Rich mama's boy.'

Suddenly I hated the masquerade of the whole deal. I knew I'd blown it and I didn't care. The stupidity of trying to hustle this woman into a dating membership had become too much trouble.

Her best sexual features were her tits, big and sloppy. Ten pounds each. At least I'd get fucked. I talked to her, but I was looking at her tits. 'Do you want to put your membership fee on your credit card or do you want to pay by check?'

'Credit card,' she slurped back.

When we began fucking, she called me angel-dick but was snoring thirty seconds after I put it in.

Chapter Sixteen

I SLEPT GOOD. I read her *Oxford Book of English Verse* and drank her whiskey until two o'clock, then nodded off. Four or five hours. In the morning, when I woke up, there was whiskey in a juice glass on the night stand by my head, and a Percodan in case of pain.

The big woman was moving around the bedroom, getting dressed for work. I watched her lean forward to flop her ponderous breasts into a red bra. I liked red bras. Sluts wore red underwear.

She caught me looking at her, while she checked herself out in the mirror. 'I joined your dating service, didn't I?' she said.

'You're a full member of DMI.'

'Was it worth it?'

'Buyer's remorse?'

'You're a fuck monster.'

A dream I'd had that night came back to me. In it, Jonathan Dante was rowing a boat alone. Tara's tits made me think of the dream. The boat. I was swimming alongside as he rowed. The great ocean was calm and clear and only my father and I were present. From time to time, I looked over at him, but he never acknowledged me and he never stopped rowing. It was a repeating dream. I'd had it over and over for years. It usually ended with him rowing away and disappearing in the boat.

It was the first time I'd had the dream since Dante died. This time, I was alone in the water. Dante was gone.

I thought to myself that now I was beginning to know what it is like to have lost my father and to have nothing that could ever replace that loss. The idea fell on my heart like a cold, sopping blanket. I had loved him and not known it. The fullness of the pain invaded me and stopped my breath. I swallowed a sob.

His dreams were gone. The unread stories and books he'd written that meant life to him would never be published. He would never know recognition. The beauty and purity of his words and dreams had died deep within him. His storm against God and life was over. He had been a real artist, an original human being. No one would ever know.

It made me want to write for him. To put something down that would sell well enough that people would see it, and I would be able to tell them to read my father, a real writer, a true poet, lost and great and beautiful. Jonathan Dante.

Tara was saying to me, 'Will I see you again?'

It took a few seconds to make my mouth work. 'I'll be back tonight with five videos of eligible single adult men,' I said.

She left for work, trusting me enough to leave me in her bedroom and let me get up and dress on my own time.

Just as the door closed behind her and I was alone, a bad thought jumped up. I'd forgotten to call in. Berkhardt was strict about discipline and phoning. He'd made a big point about it in the training.

I rolled to her side of bed to get the phone and a squirt of sourness twisted my throat. I drank the whiskey left in the juice glass and went to the kitchen. The whiskey was gone, but in the refrigerator was a six pack of Black Cherry Cisco Wine Coolers. I took two back to the bedroom with me.

When I'd finished them and taken the Percodan, I dialed the DMI number.

The DMI message system answered – the penalty for calling in at an off-hour. I pressed 'one' for English then I was made to listen to a list of current singles activities, another one of names and numbers of couples giving parties, and finally an invitation to a 30% discount for this month only to members who got a friend to join.

When I finally got to the menu that allowed me to spell in the name of the person I wanted to talk to, I pushed in the letters B E R K . . . and was connected to my boss's extension.

'This is Bruno Dante calling in,' I began. 'I must have dialed wrong when I called my results in last night . . . I was probably confused. Anyway, I'm calling back now . . . I have an excellent report to communicate. Outstanding, even. My client, Ms. Kerns in Redondo Beach, has decided to join DMI. Paid in full. Additionally, Ms. Kerns wanted me to say to my boss that she will be writing a letter telling him, you, how I have assisted in transforming her dating life . . . She said I should have been a psychotherapist . . . I'll be bringing her credit card payment and paperwork in with me to the afternoon meeting . . .' (This, of course, was all lies except for the enrollment information.) 'By the way, Mr. Berkhardt, that's a sensational message setup we have to answer incoming calls at DMI. It's really exciting how technology can trap a caller – like holding a kitty under water – Wonderful. Outstanding. All that information we can dispense before they're allowed any options whatever. Just super!'

After showering, and shaving with one of Tara's pink disposable razors, I was fully okay and feeling the Cisco and the painkiller. I left her door unlatched, and went down to get Rocco out of the car.

He was in a lousy mood from being left alone all night. As I walked him, I could see that his limp was worse and to move his rear legs at all caused him pain. Since I was pleased with the effects of my morning Percodan, when we got inside, I located the vial in the bathroom medicine cabinet and crushed up half of one for him and mixed it in a bowl of Black Cherry Cisco Wine Cooler.

For good measure, I took another one myself and put a few spares in my pocket for later.

There was egg salad in the refrigerator. I scooped out a gob on my finger and smelled the stuff, trying to make Rocco taste it first. He refused, so I put it away. I had two more Ciscos while I watched TV. Snooping, I opened the cabinet under the set and discovered a few dozen videos of old movies. James Bond, *ET*, even an original Bogey. On the bottom shelf was an unlabeled video box without the usual glossy jacket, plain black. I opened it up and found a sticker on the inside of the container. *Dick & Darlene Do Debbie*.

I plugged the movie into the VCR.

It was good. Good color and good action with lots of close-ups of Dick's enlarged wang penetrating Darlene and Debbie.

Debbie was young and reminded me a lot of Susan Bolke, with the same blond, frizzy hair and pretty eyes. Of the three participants she was the most active and original.

Ten minutes into the movie, my dick was hard and I was feeling whacked from the wine cooler and the dope, and hungry all at the same time. The Percodan had done a good job on Rocco, too, and he was resting comfortably on the carpet next to the couch. The idea of the egg salad now appealed to me.

In the kitchen, I again peeled back the plastic sheet that covered the bowl of mashed-up egg and celery and mayonnaise with little slivers of green onion. I sampled the stuff with a spoon. It was okay. Flat and without personality, but satisfactory.

I returned to the living room with the bowl, some salt and crackers and the last of the Ciscos. I ate and watched the movie.

On the TV, Darlene was doing Dick while Debbie jerked off using a shiny chrome dildo. In and out. In and out. I decided to beat off with her, move for move, so I set my food aside.

When I was ready to come, the thought of unifying my spirit with Tara made me ejaculate on top of the remaining mixture of egg salad in the bowl. I fantasized the big woman eating it with crackers or on toast, and my orgasm was intensified.

When I was done, I polished off the last of my Cisco and folded the plastic wrap back over the top of the bowl and pulled it tight, just like I'd found it. Then I carefully put the bowl back in the refrigerator on the top shelf in the place where it had been.

In the bedroom, I sat down on Tara's bed for a minute to rest my eyes, and woke up three hours later. I didn't want to be late for the sales meeting, so I quickly went back and put all the Cisco Black Cherry bottles in the trash and rinsed Rocco's bowl in the sink. Then, making sure the door was secure and locked, the dog and I left the condo with my DMI video demo kit.

As I crossed the street with Rocco, I noticed that he wasn't limping. The painkiller had worked. It felt good to be doing something nice for the dog.

I arrived at the sales meeting on time, holding Tara's full-pay contract in my hand. The other sales guys looked impressed. It was a good moment; one demo, one deal. But Berkhardt scanned me up and down with disapproving eyes as he accepted my paperwork.

The sale, it turned out, was less important than me being out of uniform. I was rebuked, instead of complimented, in front of the other trainees. No tie!

I'd left Tara's condo so concerned about locking the door behind me, that in the process, I'd forgotten the fucker in her bedroom or on her living room couch. My one-pay cash deal was negated by my appearance. Obedience to procedures was more important to Berkhardt.

While I stood singled out before the other six new robots, we were instructed on the importance of following directions and sticking fast to DMI's success formula. Berkhardt was making sure that his marketing force adhered to the McDonald's hamburgers' cookie-cutter, stencil-style winning formula that had made DMI a rich company. I was the fall-guy.

After his twenty-five-minute discourse, Berkhardt finally held my deal up, 'Outstanding job, Dante,' he said. 'One out of one!'

Some of the guys clapped, some didn't, unsure of what the boss expected of them. It wasn't much of an 'atta boy.'

'Tell us how it happened, Dante,' Berkhardt insisted.

I was out of gas, feeling deflated. 'I just did what I was told, and followed the presentation outline, Mr. Berkhardt,' I said.

'Exactly right!' he bellowed. 'We stick to established winning procedures and hold precisely to what's worked to create success. We're not reinventing the wheel here. A track-record of success is nothing to argue with. Right, Dante?'

'Right, Mr. Berkhardt.'

'You know, Bruno, Mitch Glickman pulled down eighty grand his first year by following the DMI success formula. He did whatever it took to insure that his income would be in the top two percent of the population of the United States. If that meant doing an extra demo each day, then that's what Mitch did. He came in early and stayed late. But his success began with the simple things like wearing a tie and a clean shirt, and calling in at the end of each appointment. The fundamentals. Right, Dante?'

'Right.'

On our way out, as we filed passed, Berkhardt pulled me aside and closed the conference room door. 'Dante,' he hissed, 'what's up? What's your fucking problem?'

'I'm ready,' I said, 'I think I can do two deals tonight. But I need to discuss the possibility of an advance. I'm a bit short.'

'Cut the crap! Sit down.'

'One demo, one deal. I'm your new Mitch Glickman, boss.' I sat down. 'What's on your mind, Mr. Berkhardt?'

'Nobody said you couldn't sell. I knew that when you walked into my office. But slick answers won't get it done at DMI. We're looking for winners. I was wrong about you, Dante. You're a saboteur. You've got an ax in your hand and you're hacking a hole in your own life raft. You're on your way down, not up. You're a waste, Bruno. A loser.'

The remark angered me. 'Untrue,' I snapped, 'you saw what I can do. I'm committed.'

'You're committed to piss! Walking in here half-tanked, in a wrinkled dress shirt with no tie. What do you think I'm running, a housekeeping service? Fuck you! You're bullshitting a bullshitter. You're sitting here right now, working me because you're afraid of losing a paycheck.'

'Let's not forget that I made the only sale yesterday.'

'Not true. Mitch closed two out of two.'

'I'm talking about the trainees. New people.'

'Somewhere in you, in our job interview, I saw a hotshot salesman with ability, but he's so deeply imbedded up your ass that it would take Roto Rooter and a firehose enema to get you to take a shit and let him out. You're high maintenance, Dante.'

'What you saw inside me was not a hotshot salesman, it was

a vampire. But your jive weekly guaranteed income program can't compensate me enough to endure your weak limp-dick reprimands. I'm making this company money. Maybe I didn't earn any style points today, but I showed up here with the horns and the tail. That's what you and your boss take to the bank. Let's tell it like it is.'

I knew I'd pissed him off. He was in my face. 'I don't need drinkers with personal problems on my staff,' he yelled. 'I sure as shit don't need you. Plain English, FUCK YOU!'

He reached into his pocket and pulled out a roll of hundred dollar bills, peeling off two. He handed those to me. 'Your bonus check for the other $200 will be ready on Friday. You're fired!'

I sized him up, watching his eyes, thinking for an instant that I might still be able to intimidate him. But I could see that this wasn't a bluff . . . 'Wait!' I said finally, wanting to save the job, 'I'm sorry.'

'You're bumped! I said take a walk!'

'Why not try being fair?'

'Fuck fair! You embarrassed yourself in front of my crew and you think I should blow in your ear? You've got your money. We're even. You're gone!'

'I said that I made a mistake . . . I want another chance.'

'You're a piccolo, Dante. A smart-mouthed juice mooch. I missed it at the interview and in the sales training, but I see it now.'

'It's true, I had a drink. I was celebrating the sale. Let me prove that I can do this job.'

'What you are is a taker, mister. A user. That's your thing. You said it, a vampire. You've got nothing at stake here. You're too quick and slick for DMI.'

'It won't happen again. I guarantee it.'

Berkhardt extended his hand. He had calmed down. 'Let's

both quit while we're ahead. No hard feelings. I wish you Merry Christmas and good luck.'

We did not shake. I'd been fired many times from better jobs. This time I didn't have the energy to walk away. 'I'm asking for my job back,' I said, meeting Berkhardt's eyes.

'I get twenty guys a month through here, Dante. Sometimes thirty. That's a lot of plastic dress shirts and clip-on ties over a two year period. I've become a pretty good fortune teller about salesmen. Human nature. I'm going to tell you what I've noticed. Are you interested in a little free advice?'

'Sure.'

'I've noticed that some guys learn life's shitty little lessons through experience. Repetition. There's a specific type, like me. We fail, then we get up and try again. Somewhere in me, I know that if I hang on long enough, I can usually break through my resistance, come out the other side. I can be teachable. It takes time, but I can usually learn to understand another way. I don't have to be bleeding from the eyes to get the point. I'm a worker bee. A plodder. A drone. My kind make it to the finish line.

'You're not that type. You're the other kind. You're a quick study. You're smart and you ring the bell right away. In a flash you're on top, off and running, the master of the hundred-yard dash. The problem that your type has is that you don't listen and you keep insisting on operating by your own rules. Only you push and shove and wiggle and spit and outsmart everybody. You're a lover of man and beast alike, as long as you're getting your way. With people like you, Bruno, pain is the only teacher. Failure. No one can tell you that you're about to put your hand in a buzz saw. But it's only when you, yourself, see fingertips flying past your eyes, and watch your arm being chopped into a bloody stump that you'll be able to stop. You hit all walls full speed. That's what I mean by high maintenance.'

'Let me try it again, Mr. Berkhardt. I'll do a good job. I'll be teachable. I need the gig.'

He could see I was serious. 'Why should I? You'll just blow it. You're a bad risk, Bruno.'

'I'm tired.'

He looked at me intently. 'Fuck up once more and you're gone. Agreed?'

'No problem.'

Chapter Seventeen

WITH THE TWO hundred dollars, I put gas in the Dart and checked under the hood. With oil, it came to twenty bucks. Then Jonathan Dante's dog and I went to Thrifty's Drug Store in Marina del Rey and bought all name brands: Six pints of Jack Daniels and two cartons of Marlboro Red. I got a two-hundred-and-fifty-pill size of Tylenol for me and the dog, for when the Percodans ran out, a large bag of Fritos and magazines – *People. Time. Newsweek.* Then I got six cans of the most expensive dog food in the store, men's hair spray (because I'd never tried it), a few paperback novels, three polyester dress shirts marked medium, a new clip-on tie, deodorant and Old Spice after shave. When I cashed in at the counter, I counted the paper money. I had twenty-two bucks left.

I loaded the stuff and the dog in the car and drove to the beach in Playa del Rey, passing the acres of undeveloped swampland west of Lincoln Boulevard, where Culver Boulevard dead-ends at the ocean. There, I parked the Dart in a big empty lot with a padlocked ticket booth. The chain was down and no attendant was on duty so I pulled right up, as far as I could, to the wide, white beach.

Winters in L.A. keep the shoreline temperature in the fifties and sixties, and, since this stretch of coast was no good for surfing, I was alone. I stayed in the car and let Rocco loose, while I opened the Fritos and cracked a new pint of Jack and started reading the first paperback novel.

The corn chips were good and salty but I was unable to get beyond the second page of the book because of the piss-poor writing style. My old man's intolerance for bad writing had rubbed off on me. I thought, shit, I can do this! I can write better than this! Unable to go on, I flung the book into the back seat.

When I looked around, Rocco was out of trouble down the beach, hobbling after a sea gull.

The purchase of the next novel had been a gamble. I'd gotten suckered in by the blurb on top and the name of its author: 'Fifteen weeks on the Best Seller List.' Seven hundred pages. Stanley King. Page one lost me immediately, but I tried more pages, hoping to catch the balls of the book. Finally, I threw it away too.

I had a hunger to read something worth reading, to be spoken to by someone talking the truth. Remembering a used bookstore on Venice Boulevard where, when I was in high school, I had first found Hubert Selby's *Last Exit To Brooklyn*, I decided to drive by, hoping the place was still there.

I called to Rocco and folded the Fritos bag closed. It took the old pooch a minute of me clapping my hands and calling until he could get to his feet and limp back to the car. It pained me to watch him.

I went up Culver, then east on Centinela then right on Venice Boulevard. I was there in five minutes.

Without looking up, the guy behind the counter said they were out of Selby. So I took my time and nosed around in Hemingway and Saul Bellow. Nothing grabbed me.

The counter man knew books. When I asked about e.e. cummings he barked out the shelf and row. He was a reader and knew his inventory.

I found the cummings, but it was the wrong mood. I tried Bukowski. It was okay but I couldn't grab on. Finally, giving up, I turned and headed past the counter, when something made me think of my father. I'd stopped asking the question in bookstores years before, because the answer had always been the same. Something made me try again. 'Ever hear of Dante? Jonathan Dante?'

He smiled. His proud brain must have catalogued every title in the store. 'We have one of his books. D-a-n-t-e. Right?'

'Right. Which book?'

'Follow me.'

I trailed him back to a small separate area of the fiction section that seemed reserved for rare and out of print books. I hadn't noticed the special designation sign, COLLECTORS' FICTION. Immediately, I spotted an original translation of *Demian* by Herman Hesse, out of print at least forty years. Then he pointed and I saw one of my father's old paperbacks leaning against Hemingway's *A Movable Feast*, like two beleaguered soldiers in shabby uniforms. Tired and lonely. Both books were the same size.

He pulled out *Ask The Wind* and handed it to me. I held the skinny volume in my hand, trying to remember when I'd read it last. Five years? Ten? I'd lost my own personal copy long ago. I'd even forgotten that a paperback existed. The hard cover edition had been the big seller, three thousand copies, and was the only one my father had retained copies of. The smaller version was extinct immediately.

After he handed me the book, the clerk walked away. Over his shoulder, he said, 'If you want it, it's twenty-nine ninety-five. Only original Dante paperback we've ever had. Very rare.'

It was unpretentious and light in my hand. When I opened it, the spine crackled. The pages were hard and dry. This was all that was left of my father.

I began to read. About the Mexican girl and her sandals

and the young, broke writer wanting to impress her, to fall in love . . . spilling the coffee on the table top over the nickel. Page after page, each line read like the singing from a Latin high mass.

The honesty was as painful as I remembered. My father's strong exposed heart was everywhere. This novel was Dante's masterpiece, written before the fat screenwriting paychecks from Hollywood had turned him into a par golfer and a bitter old shit.

I wanted to yell out, to share this, to make sure another living person knew who the writer was who'd fashioned the experience on these pages, the greatness of this work. If his book were being read I'd be doing something for my father. There would be two people reading his work. Two might be four.

The store was empty, except for the clerk.

'Have you read this?' I called to the guy, ten yards away, up front by the register. I held the book above my head.

'Is that the Hemingway?' he yelled back.

'No. Dante. *Ask The Wind*.

'No.'

I brought it forward to the counter with me, holding the slender volume as though it were my father's ashes. I handed it to the young clerk. He was on the phone, but put the call on hold. 'This is better than Hemingway,' I said.

'I don't know Dante's stuff,' he said. 'But I've read all of Hemingway. I think *The Old Man And The Sea* is the finest piece of American fiction.'

'If you like Hemingway, this will change how you think about writing. It'll kick your ass. It still kicks mine.'

He looked at me skeptically. He was the expert. He knew the inventory. I was wasting his time. He whispered for effect, 'Sir, Ernest Hemingway was a very great writer.'

'I know Hemingway,' I said, 'you're right, he was wonderful. Dante has – had – a different kind of power. Driven. Honest. In-your-face kind of writing.'

The kid was unconvinced. 'I'll get to it someday,' he said, setting the thin volume down on the counter, nodding at the blinking hold button on his phone. 'Are you buying this? . . . Twenty-nine ninety-five.'

The original price of *Ask The Wind* was printed in bold in the upper right-hand corner of the cover as part of the artwork, '25 cents.'

His dismissive attitude pissed me off. I held the book up and pointed to the cover price. 'How much did you say?'

'It's a rare collector's item. The owner of the store sets the value. He prices all the scarce editions. I know, the owner is my father.' He picked the book up and opened the cover, pointing at the penciled-in price on the inside. 'See,' he said, 'twenty-nine ninety-five.'

'I'll take it,' I said. 'But let me ask you something; I can see you're busy – I'll buy the book now and take it home . . . but when I'm done, if I bring it back, will you borrow it and read it?'

'Why?'

'Because it *is* better than Hemingway, goddammit! I want you to find out for yourself.'

The remark made him suspicious. This kid was cynical and oversold like everybody else in America. 'Look,' he said, 'I'm in school. I don't have a lot of free time now. Do you want this book or not?'

'What about contempt prior to investigation? You might be holding something very important in your hand! All that I'm saying is that this is great fiction.'

He rang it up. 'The total is thirty-two forty-three. Are you buying this or not?'

Having it was as important to me as breathing. 'Absolutely,' I said. 'I'm not leaving without it.'

He watched as I dug in my pocket for my money. Suddenly, it came to me that I might not have enough. I'd spent like a extravagant putz at the drug store, impulsively, scooping up throw-away junk that I'd never need.

The paper dollars were wadded and stuck together in a clump as they came out. They hit the counter with my change, and scraps of notes I'd written to myself, my comb, match books and a couple of ballpoint pens – a fistful of shit.

I did my best to separate, unwrinkle, and count at the same time, mouthing the total as I went. I had twenty-three dollars and fifty-four cents, coins and all.

'I'm short, about nine bucks,' I said. 'I haven't got enough with me.'

He'd observed the process like an admitting cop at the county jail drunk tank. I'd kept his *on-hold* call waiting too long. 'I can see that . . . just leave me a deposit and come back when you have the balance. I'd be willing to set the book aside for you.'

'No, I don't want to do that.'

Now he was openly disgusted. He turned from me and punched the hold button on his phone and petulantly addressed the caller on the other end of the receiver. 'May I get back to you?' he said into the phone. 'It seems we have a situation here.'

He then hung up.

'Okay,' he said, facing me, folding his arms, 'do you want to pay by check?'

'No.'

'Look sir, we have no mind reading section here. Your total is $32.43 with tax. What do you want to do?'

It was then that I remembered my wife's Visa credit card.

I knew it was void and shit – useless but I hoped that because the purchase was inexpensive, that he might not run it through his verification process. 'What about plastic? You take that, right?'

'Of course,' he said, as if I were a senile geriatric, 'Visa and Master and American Express. Why didn't you say so?'

'I forgot that I had the card with me.'

After I handed him the plastic he checked the expiration date. I knew that the card looked completely valid. But his interaction with me must have annoyed him enough to follow the full procedure, because he swiped the card anyway. I was screwed.

Thirty seconds later, I could see the readout as it moved across the little computer window next to the register in a trail of bold green block letters, 'Invalid Card . . . Invalid Card . . . Invalid Card.' His machine didn't give the reason.

'What's the problem?' I said, sure I was busted, and ready like a thief to snatch the book and run from the store.

He was reexamining the card. 'I don't know . . .' Then he looked up – he'd read the embossed letters on the face. 'Your name's Dante too! Bruno Dante.' He held it up. 'Are you related to Jonathan Dante? The Dante that wrote this book?'

I felt shame, exposure. I hadn't wanted him to know. My praise for my father's writing had been excessive and now, because of my relationship, the clerk would probably reject my opinion of the excellence of the book. I nodded yes. 'He was my father,' I said, experiencing the fullness of the heat in my face.

'Your card's no good . . . what do you want to do?'

I couldn't stop. I had to take a chance . . . I wanted the book and there was nothing to lose. 'He just died a few days ago,' I said, lowering my voice. 'It's been years since I've seen a copy of *Ask The Wind*. It's his best book. I lost my only copy a long time ago.'

The register kid was wearing hip, wire-framed, gold glasses and a long-sleeved plaid shirt that they sell in Westwood in men's boutiques near the UCLA campus. This was an arrogant college smart-ass brat, a know-it-all.

His eyes had changed. 'My father has a lung tumor. Cancer,' he said, his eyes fixed on the cash register's keys. 'I've been in charge of this store for three months while he's on chemo. He won't be coming back.'

He then swept the money from the counter into his hand. 'How much did you say was here?'

I said, 'Twenty-three dollars.'

'Sold . . . take the book.'

Chapter Eighteen

AFTER PICKING UP my leads at the Dream Mates International office, I swung by Tara Kerns' condo, dropping off five videos of eligible single males and borrowing $100 until pay day. We had a few drinks first, and Tara made me promise to come back later. She walked me to the Dart and I introduced her to Rocco. She pretended to think he was cute.

My 6:00 p.m. lead was in Venice. On 26th Avenue. A remodeled craftsman house built before 1920. Number eighteen. Mrs. Nancy Cooper.

I arrived early, parked around the corner, and sat outside in the car smoking, sipping from a pint of Jack and reading my copy of *Ask The Wind*.

I had a good feeling about this demo. I was keeping my word to Berkhardt. The collar of my clean new shirt was scraping my neck and my new clip-on tie was neat and in place.

At 5:59 p.m. I walked up the concrete steps and knocked on the thick, wood front door.

Nancy was in her late sixties; but plastic surgery, suction and the reconstruction of her ass, face and breasts had reduced her sags and made her appear much younger. She answered the door in pink, skin-tight sweat pants and a matching cutoff T-shirt that exposed her tanned tummy. Her hair was white-blond and her lipstick matched the pink 'CA' logo ironed on the front of the shirt.

When she said, 'Hi honey, c'mon in,' it ruined the whole

deal. The voice was derived from a throat and lungs that had chain-smoked for fifty years. Hearing her sandpaper voice made me think of Lucille Ball. She could easily have been a character out of *Ask The Wind*. My mind was bringing the residue of Jonathan Dante's book into the house with me. I'd read the first fifty pages in less than half an hour, breathing life into myself with each phrase. Each comma.

I followed Nancy into the living room, watching her spiked heels as they jabbed the Persian rug. I was hauling my presentation materials and videos under my arm, amused by the realization that this woman was only a couple of years younger than my own mother. I admired her desire to stay attractive and young, and I could already see that those characteristics might easily be used to convince her to join DMI. I was feeling the potential of my second sale.

Nancy had money. Her place had been professionally decorated. There was original artwork everywhere, and the walls of the living room had been upholstered in what looked like raw silk.

My hostess sat down opposite me on one of the two pink leather sofas, and scooped up a pack of Camel filter cigarettes and a lighter from the mirrored coffee table. 'I smoke,' she rasped in pure Bronxese.

'No problem,' I said. Thinking that I was establishing customer rapport, I took a book of matches from my pocket, lit her cigarette, and my own too.

Also on the table was a tall crystal glass half-full of red wine or liqueur. 'Drink? Beer?' she asked, nodding at her glass.

'What you're having looks fine. I'll have that.'

'An after-dinner drink. Sweet.'

'Sounds good.'

Nancy called over her shoulder. 'Elpedia, un otro vaso con el mismo para el senor. Rapido, por favor. Inmediatamente!'

A fat Mexican woman poked her head out of the kitchen. 'Okay, Señora Cooper.'

We started right off on the DMI questionnaire. I asked my preliminary stuff while I let her work her way down the form.

My drink came on a tray with a half-full bottle of Bristol Cream. Elpedia set it down with a coaster. I sipped my glass while she finished up the form.

When Nancy handed the clipboard back, I could see that she'd skipped a lot of the boxes, mostly neglecting the personal preference section. So I started asking the questions she hadn't answered. 'What type of potential lifetime partner appeals to you?' I read from my sheet. 'You can be general or specific.'

She looked annoyed. 'The luvva type, what else?'

'Okay,' I said, checking the appropriate box, 'but could you be a bit more specific?'

'I travel to PV and Cancun four times a year. A nice Mexican boy. Pretty. Taller than me. Central American would be okay. Twenty-five to thirty. Education, etcetera, isn't important, but I like a good swimmer. The athletic type is nice.'

I was making notes, checking more boxes, finishing my first glass of sherry. I poured myself another, and topped off Nancy's glass.

She went on. 'Somebody who smokes or doesn't mind if I do.'

Remembering my conversation with Berkhardt, I continued sticking with the presentation, reading from the next section, but I could tell that the questions were out of sync with my client's interest level. 'Nancy, please list the important things that you would like to have in common with your dream mate?'

The inquiry brought a grin from Mrs. Cooper, and a laugh-cough that went on for several seconds. 'What interests would you guess?'

I laughed, too, but my answer was to gain control and bring Nancy down to earth. 'We're talking about a forty-year age difference,' I said.

She lit another cigarette, then threw her lighter on the table. 'Let's cut to the finish part, honey, the ass-end! I'm a direct kind of person. What I want is a companion, a sweetie pie. That's what I told the phone girl when we talked yesterday. I like 'em young and his not having money is no problem. He wouldn't even need a job because I've got enough for the two of us. If you want, I could employ him as my houseboy. What I like about Dream Mates is the video part. I can order what I want and not screw around with losers. You're here to show me videos. Do your job.'

Her arrogance hooked me and my mouth began moving without orders from my brain. 'Nancy,' I said, 'there's a difference between an escort service and a dating service.'

'You're right. I bet yours charges a whole lot more.'

'DMI isn't in the wetbacks-stud business. Try Venice Boulevard or a Salsa club in Hollywood.'

Her purse was out and on the coffee table. 'How much? Are we doing business or what?'

The conversation was over. It didn't matter if it was a tit job or a tummy tuck, the money was on the table and I knew enough to shut up. To Nancy, I was there like a servant delivering pizza. An order taker.

'Make your check out to Dream Mates International,' I said. 'You've got my guarantee that whomever you're paired with will have pubic hair and possibly even a third-grade education.'

Mrs. Cooper squashed out her cigarette. 'I pay cash,' she growled, extracting a handful of hundred-dollar bills. 'I said, how much?'

'Two thousand dollars.'

She counted out twenty hundred-dollar bills. 'I want a receipt too. Skip the rest of the crap.'

I set my presentation case with the five videos on the table and stroked a big 'X' at the bottom of a contract. Then I slid my pen, the case, and the form across to her. 'Starter videos and agreement with guarantee. Sign there at the bottom.'

Berkhardt would be pleased. I'd done my second deal.

I immediately visited the liquor store after Mrs. Cooper's. The one on the corner of Venice Boulevard and Pacific. The Bristol Cream and the demo had given me a taste for wine. Mad Dog wine.

After I got a gallon jug, I drove the few blocks to where Washington Boulevard meets Venice Pier. Again, there was no attendant in the ticket booth so I pulled into the big, open parking lot near the stairs at the base of the pier. I had an hour and a half to go before my next presentation, but it didn't matter because I'd made up my mind to quit my job.

Rocco was worse. Two times over the past few days he'd lost control of his bowels and crapped, first on the rear seat, then on the floorboard of the Dart. Now he'd been yowling continually from the pain.

Before getting out of the car, I poured some Mad Dog in his bowl and forced him to swallow a Percodan by putting it far back at the top of his throat, the way they did to unconscious or restrained patients at the recovery unit. The pooch gagged, then lapped up the wine.

The December night wasn't cold, but the air was wet and heavy, soaked by the salty odor of the Pacific. I let Rocco walk on the sand until he crapped, while I sat on a concrete bench that was lit only from the light of the old biker bar, the Sunset Saloon. When he was done, the dog came and sat at my feet. Twenty-five yards away we could hear the waves popping. I patted him gently. 'Sorry, bud,' I whispered. 'I know it hurts.'

For a long time, I sat and sipped from the jug, staring into the blackness, trying to concentrate on what to do next with my life. The longer I sat, the more I was filled with anger and self-contempt. It took many deep pulls on the bottle before I could feel my head begin to slow down.

I hated Dream Mates International. I could no longer put on a sport coat and tie, and invent concern while dipping my hands into the bank accounts of people who'd convinced themselves that what their life lacked was the fix of a quality dating service. I was having the same feelings I'd had when I quit telemarketing – taking money from mooches for too many years. I was done. Price too high.

Twenty hundred-dollar bills of DMI's money filled my front pants pocket. I felt like throwing the wad into the ocean, or keeping the whole fee for myself. Driving north to San Francisco, or back to New York. DMI's only record of Bruno Dante was a motel address in Hollywood. Fuck 'em. And fuck crazy Nancy Cooper.

Two hours before, I had reread fifty pages of *Ask The Wind*. Something had been awakened when I had set the book down. After not reading it in so many years the sudden reflection of my father's honesty, and the sheer poetry of the writing shamed me. I felt disgraced by my own selfishness. My failure as a writer.

While my father had been alive, *Ask The Wind*, too, was alive. But that was no more. A great unknown writer was silenced. I could have been a writer like Jonathan Dante. I had ability once. Yet I had quit too, the way he quit and sold himself to the film business.

I might even have written books. He had done it. Why hadn't I? It was because I had given up, had never had the courage to let myself fail. My father was dead, and so was I. That was the sadness and the truth that was in my soul.

I craved conversation. Companionship. Half-drunk and halfway down on my jug, I decided to go in and have a belt at the Sunset Saloon. Maybe buy some of the bikers at the bar a shooter.

I rose from the bench, thinking of the money in my pants. My wealth. I took Rocco's collar and started for the door, when I remembered what I was wearing, my absurd business attire: the sport coat and ridiculous clip-on tie. I was a fraud. I fit nowhere. I sat back down and yanked the tie off my stiff new shirt and began using it to play tug-of-war with my dog.

Presently, I heard voices. Faint at first. Then, coming slowly out of the darkness of the foggy air of the Strand, I saw two dudes shuffling in my direction. As they approached, I began to make out that they were arguing loudly in a language that was not American. Spanish. Day laborers or farm workers. Fellow outdoorsmen.

They approached slowly because their on-going argument necessitated making frequent stops. The quarreling came in puffed combinations of mumbles and snarls and indecipherable Spanish syllables. They'd halt, one would jab the other in the chest with a finger, or wave his arms wildly until his point was resolved, then they'd continue on.

When they got closer, I could tell that they were on a wine-drunk like me. When they shuffled nearer my bench, I held the clip-on tie in my fist to stop them and extended it out, blocking their way.

The taller of the two men, the worse for his wine, seemed to be the bolder. He stopped, evaluated my offer without words, then, slowly coming to the realization that my submission was free, he grabbed at the tie and missed.

I handed it to his partner, and a loud discussion in Spanish and a pushing match followed, until they determined who would own the knotted and chewed cloth. The shorter man, wearing a filthy hooded sweatshirt and sporting a recent cut, high on his cheek, held tight to the tie and slapped it to his chest, even making an attempt to hook it over the zipper at the top of his sweatshirt.

I got up and stuck my bottle of Mad Dog between them. We all sat down immediately and took a hit.

They were drunker than I, but good drinkers. We passed the jug back and forth and the tie soon became a bandage to be used to soak up blood from the face wound of the smaller guy.

I knew a hundred words of bad Spanish from Catholic high school, so I was able to find out the names of my friends – one was Hector, the other Ignacio.

We drank and almost finished the bottle. The idea came to me that the smaller one, Hector, would make an excellent, pre-selected date and possible traveling companion for DMI's new, rich lady client who lived in the neighborhood. By the light of street lamps, the three of us and Rocco made our way down the Strand until we came to 26th Avenue.

Hector fit only a couple of Nancy Cooper's criteria – he was Latin and he smoked. But that was good enough. I was remembering her crack about also needing a houseboy. That convinced me to make the match. Hector had said he had no job, and I was sure that he wouldn't be opposed to light chores in exchange for receiving the odd humping from Mrs. Cooper.

Me and Hector had changed shirts while standing in the sand. Ignacio held the bottle. As it turned out, the sport coat looked okay and the blood-stained tie hooked nicely back on the top and completed the ensemble.

I'd explained video dating to Hector, in broken Spanish, as well as possible, and he seemed receptive to the idea of giving Dream Mates International a whirl.

Iggy waited out of sight, while I hauled Hector up the steps and knocked on Nancy Cooper's door. The maid answered, looking through the peep hole. I thought she recognized me. She didn't see Hector because I intentionally blocked her view.

'Señora Cooper, por favor,' I said.

The peephole closed and she went away. A minute later Nancy Cooper's surgically-altered face appeared at the little door. It was oozing a thick overnight cream of some sort. 'You're back again. What do you want?'

'Mrs. Cooper, I'd like to speak to you for a moment. I have good news.'

'Are you drunk? You sound drunk. Go away.'

I was whispering. 'Mrs. Cooper, we're in luck. I think we've found a suitable Mexican adult who is available to travel, needs a job and owns his own dick.'

'What?'

'I've located someone for you to date.'

'You left the wrong videos. We'll talk about it tomorrow.'

'I know. It was an oversight.'

'Go bring me what I paid for.'

'That's why I came back. Open the door.'

'Okay. Okay. Why didn't you say so? Wait a minute. I'll go put my robe on.'

By the time she came back, I had Hector's jacket buttoned and he'd taken my place at the door.

Chapter Nineteen

THE DMI OFFICE opened every day at 10:00 a.m. When I woke up, I was laying on the front seat of the Dart, in the parking lot of Dream Mates International. I had a complete memory of the night before. This time, there had been no blackout on the Mad Dog. Closing my eyes, I tried to synchronize the throbbing in my brain with my breathing. Some homeopathic asshole had once told me it worked to reduce hangover pain. He wasn't a wine drinker.

My watch said ten forty-five. Friday. Pay day.

As I walked around the corner of the building, from her desk on the other side of the building's glass wall, Susan Bolke saw me coming and made a repulsed face. I saw myself in the glass. My sport coat and tie were replaced by the dirty red sweatshirt from the night before. She dialed somebody on the phone, then resumed chatting with a male client who had video boxes in his hand and was sitting on the corner of her desk looking down the top of her blouse.

Susan didn't acknowledge me, but continued smiling and talking to the client, so I waited. After a couple of minutes of observing her breasts seducing the customer, I understood that I was being ignored.

'Excuse me!' I said, 'I'm here to see Mr. Berkhardt.'

She gestured at the reception area without looking at me. Poisonous. 'Sit down over there. He'll be with you in a few minutes.'

I was too hungover to engage her, but I saw a stack of sealed window envelopes on her desk. The top one had the name of one of the other salesmen typed on the front. 'Is my paycheck one of those?' I asked.

Susan ignored me and went back to her conversation with the DMI mooch.

'Pardon me,' I said politely, 'may I ask a question?'

'What is it now?'

'When was the last time you let one of your boyfriends puke on your tits?'

Berkhardt's office door was closed. I didn't wait to be asked. I went in and let it swing shut behind me. 'I'm here for my paycheck,' I said. 'Not for trouble.'

He slammed down his phone and jumped up from his chair, knocking a miniature Christmas tree off the end of his desk. Berkhardt was red-faced, ready for action. I stopped him by handing him the fistful of hundred-dollar bills from the Cooper deal. Then I sat down.

His attitude changed immediately. He picked up the tree and replaced it. 'The police are looking for you,' he said.

'For what?'

He sat down too. 'Mrs. Cooper has been hysterical all morning. Calls every five minutes. She's making a lot of trouble, saying that you assaulted her. Because there was missing cash involved, I had to protect the company and make a police report.'

'I'm no criminal. Count it. It's all there.'

He fanned the money and saw I wasn't lying. 'You look like shit. What happened at Mrs. Cooper's?'

'I'm no salesman anymore. I'm done. That's what happened.'

'You were drunk. Weren't you? Shit, Dante, you're heading

right at that wall, going a hundred miles an hour. Living is fucking up your drinking.'

I got to my feet. 'I believe we're square. Have you got a paycheck for me?'

He opened his desk drawer and threw a sealed envelope on the desk in front of me. Through the plastic window I saw my name typed on the check.

Then I heard my voice say, 'Thanks for giving me a second chance. I apologize.' I extended my hand to him.

'Did you assault Mrs. Cooper?'

'No.'

He shook my hand. 'What are you going to do now?'

'I'm not sure. I used to be a writer.'

'I remember . . . I mean for money.'

'Odd jobs. Wash dishes. Work in a parking lot. Grunt stuff, whatever I need to do to pay the bills while I write again.'

'What makes you think your drinking won't interfere?'

'If it does, I'll quit.'

'Poetry, wasn't it? You've had your work published?'

'Yes.'

'I get a lot of people through here looking for a night job that pays quick money. Huge egos. Actors. Models. L.A.'s full of that. Airheads. People trying to break into TV. You're the first one who admitted to being a poet.'

'As far back as I can remember, what I wanted to do was escape from this city. To get as far from L.A. as possible. That's less important now. What I really need to be able to do is deal with my thoughts. Writing used to give me peace.

'I'll cancel the police report. It's Christmas, they're busy anyway.'

The information surprised me. 'It's Christmas?'

'December 24th.'

Chapter Twenty

I GOT OUT to the car and unlocked the driver's door. Rocco could not greet me. Unable to lift his head off the back seat, the best he could do was roll his eyes. He emitted a high-pitched moan and I could tell he was in great pain.

He'd shat again on the back seat. More liquid than solid. It ran across the bench cushion and collected in a hideous pool at the 'V' of the seat's backrest. Inhaling the stink made me turn and vomit again and again by the side of the car.

After airing out the Dart I cleaned up Rocco's shit with paper towels and tried to force a Percodan between his jaws. It was useless. He refused to cooperate and his moaning persisted.

I was afraid. It made me cringe to think he might be dying.

At a Shell gas station on Lincoln Boulevard they cashed DMI paychecks. I got my two hundred-dollar bills and began calling Vet Clinics listed in the Yellow Pages with a handful of quarters. Everything was closed. After eight or ten calls, I'd reached only answering machines.

Finally in Brentwood, on Bundy Drive, I got a live voice at a place called the Rescue Pet Clinic. A foreign-sounding receptionist said that I should hurry because they would be closing by noon.

I parked in front of the vet's office on Bundy Drive, but I was unable to bring myself to carry Rocco to the entrance.

Instead, I sat in the car and smoked, watching the door to the clinic, hoping to catch sight of a bandaged animal leaving the premises, some sign of impending doom from within to justify my not going in. None came. The only thing unusual about the place were the reminders of the nasty Northridge earthquake that could still be seen on the cracked sidewalk leading up to the house and the listing porch that gave the old, converted Victorian a twisted smile.

The Santa Anas were blowing again, and the tall palms lining either side of the street rolled in slow motion with the gusts from the east. Seventy, eighty feet high, an endless row of them, curving north past Wilshire up to San Vicente. Slender dinosaurs waving their pom-poms at a blue Christmas sky.

As I waited, I began to jot down an idea for a poem. About L.A. It felt strange but the words kept coming until most of the concept was out of my brain and on to the paper. Writing something quelled my anxiety about my dog. At eleven forty-five, in need of a drink to medicate myself, I left the poem idea in the glove compartment and carried Rocco into the vet's office.

The place was empty. Doctor Wong was the animal guy – an old Chinese veterinarian. He directed me down a hall to an examining room, where I set Rocco on a long stainless steel table with a drain at one end that resembled an embalming counter. The room had white buckled linoleum floors and reeked of nicotine.

Wong began his examination of my dog. Because of the pain, Rocco was fading in and out of consciousness. Every time he came near Rocco's back legs, the dog yelped loudly and Dr. Wong would stop. But the old guy had a good touch; he'd stroke Rocco's head gently until the pain subsided, then continue checking him. The exam was completed in five minutes.

Wong turned to me. 'This very sick dog,' he said. 'Afflicted with tumor.'

'How sick?' I asked.

'Large growth pressing on spine. Extreme pain.'

'Does he need X-rays?'

He was compassionate. 'Put dog to sleep with shot. Best thing.'

It was unthinkable. 'Rocco belonged to my father. I can't do that.'

'Dog live only twenty-four hour, maybe two day.'

'No shot. That's not an option. What else can you do to make him comfortable . . . morphine?'

'Have medication, Feldene. Take most of pain.'

'Good. Do that.'

First, he gave Rocco a syringe full of another painkiller in the area of his spine. Then, while I held Rocco's head in my hands, the old vet gently administered the Feldene by sticking a long eyedropper at the back of Rocco's throat and squirting in the brown liquid. He seemed to relax immediately. He looked up at me. His eyes were clear. Then he licked my hand and slid into sleep.

I carried Rocco back out to the reception area and lay him on the counter. 'How much do I owe you?' I asked.

Wong tallied it up. 'Ninety-eight dollar.'

'Fuck.'

I gave him a hundred-dollar bill and he dispensed my change from a thick wad in his pocket. Then he gave me the vial of Feldene and another bottle with an eyedropper built in. It had a white cap. 'What's this one?' I asked.

Wong spoke tenderly, in a whisper: 'Strong sedative. Dog sleep, not wake up. Give to animal when medicine not working to stop pain.'

I held the vial up. There was only a quarter-inch of liquid at the bottom. I attempted to hand it back, but old Doctor Wong put his hand on my shoulder. 'All things that live must also pass from life. This not bad thing. God's way.'

I didn't want Rocco to finish his life on the back seat of my car surrounded by hack fiction, cigarette butts and empty potato chip bags. I wanted him to die at Jonathan Dante's home in Malibu. He'd lived his life near the smell of his master and the things that were familiar – on the carpet in the old man's den where he would snooze while my father banged away on his typewriter hour after hour, where the sweetness of the ocean's sound and the taste of the salted air would remind him of a happier life.

I headed west on Wilshire Boulevard toward Santa Monica and the Coast Highway, looking for an open liquor store. First, I needed a drink to get level. Rocco was lying half-conscious next to me on the seat, his thick head on my thigh, breathing heavily and doped up to mask his pain. I knew he was dying.

As I drove, my knees began shaking. Slightly at first, but I knew that my discomfort would soon be acute. It had been ten hours since my last drink and my body was beginning to withdraw, abetted by a mind that was panicked about the dog.

I'd told myself and Morgan Berkhardt that I would taper off or quit entirely. I would, later. At present, my insides were in my throat, my hands were rattling, and I had to grip the steering wheel to inhibit the on-coming tremors. I made a commitment to myself to buy only a half-pint and no more. Just enough to take the edge off.

The first liquor store I stopped at on Wilshire was crowded. Because it was Friday, Christmas Eve – a half work-day before a holiday weekend – everyone was stocking up. I was afraid to leave Rocco alone for the time it would take to go in, stand in line, buy my bottle, and return. He could easily die, and I would not have been there to comfort him.

I watched the progress of the line at the cash register, through the window of the store, waiting for it to dissipate. It didn't. There was only one slow cashier for a long line of customers.

I decided to continue on and attempt to make it the twenty miles to the Malibu Pier Liquor Store hoping that my body might hold together long enough because there would be smaller crowds in Malibu. I backed the Dart out and drove away.

I'd completely miscalculated. Within ten minutes, my body revolted and the muscles in my stomach knotted. Unable to postpone my need for a drink, I pulled into the first liquor store at Pacific Coast Highway and Santa Monica Canyon.

The parking lot was full. I didn't care. I double-parked and maneuvered Rocco's head off my lap as gently as I could and went in. The first display had a quart-bottle of Jack Daniels in a Christmas-wrapped box. I grabbed it up and stepped quickly in line, holding the package to my chest to subdue the tremors.

I waited. Five back from the counter. Then four. Then two.

The last guy in front of me had a payroll check. Six hundred and change. He was buying a newspaper and chewing gum and a *People* magazine. Purchases totaling less than four bucks.

I waited. Shaking. The store clerk counted out the guy's cash. They knew each other and exchanged pleasantries while my sanity oozed from begging pores and drenched my shirt.

'One hundred . . . so you're off until New Year's? Lucky bastard.'

. . . 'Right'

'Not me, I'll be back in first thing Monday morning. Two

hundred. Two fifty. Three. Four. Unfortunately, this ain't a union liquor store. Ha-ha. Are tens and twenties okay?'

'Sure. No Problem.'

'. . . five hundred. Six hundred. Ten. Twenty. One. And thirty-two cents.'

It was over. The guy scooped his cash up off the counter, picked up his bag and moved on.

I stepped up. Self-conscious. There were ten customers behind me and my shaking was obvious. The guy to my immediate rear nudged forward carrying two twelve-packs. Pushing. I ignored it and set the gift box of Jack Daniels in front of the clerk who keyed the register. 'That's $21.95,' he announced.

I managed to wedge my fist into my pants and get my hundred-dollar bill. My fingers fished it out, because there was nothing else in the pocket. I dumped the wadded bill on the glass counter. My voice was a stutter. 'Ha-here.'

He picked the bill up and flattened it out. 'Nothing smaller?'

'That's . . . it.'

The register drawer popped open and he shook his head, then pushed my purchase to the side. 'Sorry,' he said. 'No change,' and handed me back my hundred . . . 'Next!'

My body was screaming a clear *drink or die* message. I grabbed several magazines, a fistful of candy bars and a flashlight with a lifetime battery charger off the counter, then pushed them all toward the clerk.

I wanted to speak, but I was panicked. Somehow no words would come from my mouth, only gasps and an odd throat-clicking sound a terrorized animal makes. To force a noise from inside, I had to slam my fist down on his glass counter – it crushed a Snickers candy bar.

'Fuck next!' I blurted. 'I'll take this other stuff too. Now!'

It angered the counter man. He surveyed the items. 'That's

still not enough!' he snapped. 'C'mon, move it, you're holding up the line.'

Behind me I could hear Twelve Packs mumbling impatiently. 'Wait,' I said, turning and grabbing the beer out of the guy's moist, fat, piggy hands and setting the cans on the counter. 'I'll take this too . . . and this . . .' The lady behind him had two bottles of good wine. I grabbed those and put them on the glass as well. 'I'm paying for their stuff too! I'm Santa Claus! What about now?' I insisted.

He rang the stuff up. 'Eighty-two twenty. That's enough. You made it.' He took my bill and counted out the rest of my change in singles.

As he began bagging, I saw him studying me, taking his time. When everything was packaged separately, he pushed my bag across the counter to me. 'Well, Santa,' he jeered, mocking my shakes, 'now that you've stocked up on your medicine, it looks like tonight's going to be a one-man Christmas party.'

Outside in the parking lot, I lay the bag containing the quart of Jack Daniels on the roof of the Dart while I fumbled my key into the lock and quickly checked Rocco through the window. He was okay. His chest continued moving up and down, heralding respiration.

I opened the car door and grabbed the lip of the paper bag, misjudging my grasp as I hefted it from the roof. My hand slipped and the gift box inside separated itself and scooted down the side of the car glass, bouncing against the asphalt pavement with a thud.

When I bent down, a brown whiskey puddle was already forming beneath the bottom of the box.

I got in the car and wrapped my hands under my armpits, which were immediately soaked again from a blast of sweat.

I had to decide; there was still money in my pocket. I could go back in again, get in line and wait, or I could stop further on toward Malibu. Going on would save seeing the clerk's gloating sneer when I ordered another bottle. But that didn't matter. I would have gone back in but Rocco eased his snout on top of my thigh, making me afraid of jarring him by my sliding out again across the seat.

Instead, I reached in the brown bag and found a Snickers.

Tearing the paper off with my teeth, I pushed the candy bar from the bottom until half of it was in my mouth. Then the other half.

The sugar blast helped. Inside my guts the clawing, drowning, screaming rat calmed slightly.

I pulled another Snickers out of the bag and gobbled that too. In a minute, enough of the edge was off that I felt like I could continue on up the highway and not have to go back in again and brave the cocky sneer of the clerk. Able to guide the key into the ignition, I started the Dart.

It took me four more Snickers to make it to Sunset and the Coast Highway. Eating and ripping the wrappers off with one hand, I drove with the other. The shaking was bad, but not out of control. I'd set my will on getting Rocco home to Point Dume, making sure that he died in my father's house. It was six more miles from Sunset to the Malibu Pier liquor store. There were two candy bars left. I told myself that I could make it and ripped one open with my mouth.

As I drove, I tried to eat as slowly as possible. The heat and moisture from my body had the candy melting fast, but I kept the wrapper on and squeezed my fist from the bottom of the bar, forcing the contents to ooze past my lips. The first one went fast. I tried to conserve the second. I waited as long as I could, and when my stomach would begin to knot, I'd take a bite.

At Topanga Canyon, Rocco started groaning loudly, and I

had to pull over. His breathing had become hard and uneven. I slid across the seat and lifted his head fully on my lap. As I stroked him, I felt his body stiffen with pain. He was dying.

I got out the eyedropper and the medicine. Without letting go of the Snickers, I used my free hand to hold the bottle, while I dipped the eyedropper in.

His head was tilted up and I shoved the point of the tube into the corner of his mouth, squirting in the painkiller. I did it a few times until he swallowed.

Then he startled me by opening his mouth. A smudge of chocolate from my fingers had clung to his dry nose, and, slowly, a wide, pink tongue came out and reached up to lick off the brown goo. I set the bottle down and held up the hand with the melted candy. Out came the tongue again as I squeezed up the Snickers. It was half-hearted, but he did it several times. Then we took turns. A bite for me, a lick for him.

I had the thought that since my chocolate had worked for Rocco, that maybe his medicine would work on me. So I took a hit from the bottle. A small one. It was hideous shit. Non-alcoholic.

When the last Snickers was gone, I slid back behind the wheel keeping his head on my lap. The candy wrapper was next to his nose.

I watched him as I drove. He'd quit licking.

When I reached the Malibu Pier liquor store I could tell that they were busy too. I had to drive to the end of the lot to find a space.

I tried, but was unable to leave the car. Afraid to move Rocco's head from my leg. He was emitting a noise that sounded like dry strangling and stroking his body seemed to be the only thing that would comfort him. I kept it up.

A long time passed. Five minutes. People came and went

from the store carrying brown paper bags and liquor boxes. Some of the bags were wide and thick for beer, some tall for whiskey and wine.

Two guys came out with small single bags, pint size. The brown paper was twisted at the top. Short dogs. Small wine bottles. My drink.

They got in a flashy four-wheel pick-up two spaces down. It had big tires and a roll bar and spotlights on the roof. I watched through the window of the car between us, as the guy behind the wheel folded the paper down around the neck of his shortie, then unscrewed the cap and took a hit. It made me shake and my stomach cramp in pain.

The truck backed out and left the lot.

People that I'd seen going in were now coming out. I could wait no more. I had parked too close to the car on my left, so I lifted Rocco's head and maneuvered myself out from under him, sliding across the seat to the passenger side. I did it as gently as I could, but I noticed that it changed his breathing to short gasps. They scared me. As I listened, they seemed to be further and further apart.

I was trapped. Unable to get out or even slide back behind the wheel. His breathing was so faint, I knew he was on the verge of death. As delicately as possible, I hiked his head back up on my leg and waited.

More time passed. I smoked cigarettes and stroked his head. He was still breathing.

To keep my mind off myself, I took the idea I'd started outside the vet's office from the glove compartment and tried concentrating on making it into a poem.

The lines fell in effortlessly. A poem about L.A. Here's what I wrote:

The long palms work their way
down Bundy Drive
Swaying in the warm December wind
A chorus line of skinny hookers
nodding willfully
at the on-coming traffic
Blowing kisses at Santa Monica Boulevard

Their crooked heels, unwashed arms,
and the heavy odor of the street
now hold no promises, no pleasures,
L.A.'s innocence is gone forever

I saw it once though
caught a glimpse
even said hi
waving out the back window of my parents' Plymouth
But it had already been bought and sold
and was much too much in a hurry
to stop
and say goodbye

When I was done I read it over a few times. It wasn't a bad
poem. Then I thought about Jonathan Dante. It was for him
that I'd written it. I promised myself that I'd write more and
they'd be for him too.

When I reached down to pat the old dog on my lap, I
realized that he was gone. Quietly, as I wrote, he had stopped
breathing.

I sat in the car for a long time holding Rocco in my arms.
Weeping. When I finally quit my shaking was better.

In a few hours it would be midnight and I would have gone
a full day on my own without a drink. And one day could

mean two. If I stayed off the booze, I knew I'd be able to write again.

I started the Dart and headed north up the Coast Highway. There was a blueness to the ocean I had never noticed before.

Started in 1992 by **Kevin Williamson**, with help from established young authors **Duncan McLean** and **Gordon Legge**, Rebel Inc magazine set out with the intention of promoting and publishing what was seen then as a new wave of young urban Scottish writers who were kicking back against the literary mainstream. The Rebel Inc imprint is a development of the magazine ethos, publishing accessible as well as challenging texts aimed at extending the domain of counter-culture literature.

Rebel Inc Fiction

Children of Albion Rovers £5.99 pbk
Welsh, Warner, Legge, Meek, Hird, Reekie
'a fistful of Caledonian classics' **Loaded**

Rovers Return £8.99 pbk
Bourdain, King, Martin, Meek, Hird, Legge
'Pacy, punchy, state of the era' **ID**

Beam Me Up, Scotty Michael Guinzburg £6.99 pbk
'Riveting to the last page . . . Violent, funny and furious' **The Observer**

Fup Jim Dodge £7.99 hbk
'an extraordinary little book . . . as good as writing gets' **Literary Review**

Nail and Other Stories Laura Hird £6.99 pbk
'confirms the flowering of a wonderfully versatile imagination on the literary horizon'
Independent on Sunday

Kill Kill Faster Faster Joel Rose £6.99 pbk
'A modern urban masterpiece' **Irvine Welsh**

The Sinaloa Story Barry Gifford £6.99 pbk
'Gifford cuts through to the heart of what makes a good novel readable and entertaining' **Elmore Leonard**

The Wild Life of Sailor and Lula Barry Gifford £8.99 pbk
'Gifford is all the proof that the world will ever need that a writer who listens with his heart is capable of telling anyone's story' **Armistead Maupin**

My Brother's Gun Ray Loriga £6.99 pbk
'A fascinating cross between Marguerite Duras and Jim Thompson'
Pedro Almodovar

Rebel Inc Non-Fiction

A Life in Pieces Campbell/Niel £10.99 pbk
'Trocchi's self-fragmented lives and works are graphically recalled in this sensitively orchestrated miscellany' **The Sunday Times**

The Drinkers' Guide to the Middle East Will Lawson £5.99 pbk
'Acerbic and opinionated . . . it provides a surprisingly perceptive and practical guide for travellers who want to live a little without causing a diplomatic incident' **The Guardian**

Locked In the Arms of a Crazy Life: A Biography of Charles Bukowski Howard Sounes £16.99 hbk
'wonderful . . . this is the first serious and thorough Bukowski biography. An excellent book about a remarkable man' **Time Out**

Drugs and the Party Line Kevin Williamson £5.99 pbk
'essential reading for Blair, his Czar, and the rest of us' **The Face**

Rebel Inc Classics

1   Hunger Knut Hamsun £6.99 pbk
with an introduction by Duncan McLean
'Hunger is the crux of Hamsun's claims to mastery. This is the classic novel of humiliation, even beyond Dostoevsky' **George Steiner** in **The Observer**

2   Young Adam Alexander Trocchi £6.99 pbk
'Everyone should read Young Adam' **TLS**

3   The Blind Owl Sadegh Hedayat £6.99 pbk
with an introduction by Alan Warner
'One of the most extraordinary books I've ever read. Chilling and beautiful' **The Guardian**

4   Helen & Desire Alexander Trocchi £6.99 pbk
with an introduction by Edwin Morgan
'a spicily pornographic tale . . . enhanced by an elegant and intelligent introduction by Edwin Morgan' **The Scotsman**

5   Revenge of the Lawn Richard Brautigan £6.99 pbk
'His style and wit transmit so much energy that energy itself becomes the message, Brautigan makes all the senses breathe. Only a hedonist could cram so much life onto a single page' **Newsweek**

6   Stone Junction Jim Dodge £6.99 pbk
with an introduction by Thomas Pynchon
'Reading *Stone Junction* is like being at a non-stop party in celebration of everything that matters' **Thomas Pynchon**

7 The Man with the Golden Arm Nelson Algren £7.99 pbk
'This is a man writing and you should not read it if you cannot take a punch . . .
Mr Algren can hit with both hands and move around and he will kill you if you
are not awfully careful . . .' **Ernest Hemingway**

8 Snowblind Robert Sabbag £6.99 pbk
with an introduction by Howard Marks
'A flat-out ballbuster, it moves like a threshing machine with a full tank of ether.
This guy Sabbag is a whip-song writer' **Hunter S. Thompson**

9 Sombrero Fallout Richard Brautigan £6.99 pbk
'Playful and serious, hilarious and melancholy, profound and absurd . . . how
delightfully unique a prose writer Brautigan is' **TLS**

10 Not Fade Away Jim Dodge £6.99 pbk
'a book which screams off the starting blocks and just keeps accelerating'
Uncut Magazine

11 Ask the Dust John Fante £6.99 pbk
with an introduction by Charles Bukowski
'a tough and beautifully realised tale . . . affecting, powerful and poignant stuff'
Time Out

12 The Star Rover Jack London £6.99 pbk
with introductions by Hugh Collins and T. C. Campbell
'an astonishing achievement' **The Sunday Times**

13 A Walk on the Wild Side Nelson Algren £6.99 pbk
with an introduction by Russell Banks
'Mr Algren, boy you are good' **Ernest Hemingway**

14 Ringolevio Emmett Grogan £7.99 pbk
with an introduction by Peter Coyote. Published June 1999

15 The Iron Heel Jack London £6.99 pbk
with an introduction by Leon Trotsky. Published June 1999

FOR YOUR FREE REBEL INC CLASSICS SAMPLER PLEASE CALL OR WRITE TO
CANONGATE BOOKS AT THE ADDRESS BELOW.

All of the above titles are available in good bookshops,
or can be ordered directly from:

Canongate Books, 14 High Street, Edinburgh EH1 1TE
Tel 0131 557 5111 Fax 0131 557 5211
email info@canongate.co.uk
http://www.canongate.co.uk